L
DARK
FACADE

CHARLOTTE DICKSON

LOVES DARK FACADE

Author Note

Writing this book was one of the most challenging and healing experiences of my life. During the process, I faced my own mental health crisis, a time that tested me in ways I never could have imagined. If you look closely, you can see the difference in my writing. The struggles, the doubts, the hope, they're all there.

At one point, I considered rewriting the entire book, smoothing over the cracks and imperfections that mirrored my own. But I chose not to. Because to me, this book isn't just a story, it's proof. Proof that even in our darkest moments, we can create something meaningful. Proof that we can endure. That we can overcome.

Because mental health is a cause so very close to my heart, I have made a commitment. 10% of my royalties each month will be donated to a mental health charity. It's my way of giving back and helping others find light in their own journeys.

Thank you for reading, and for sharing this journey with me.

With love,

Charlotte Dickson

Trigger warnings

This book contains sensitive material relating to:

abusive relationships,
anxiety,
cheating,
child abuse,
death of a friend,
depression,
domestic violence,
drugs,
emotional abuse,
overdose,
panic attacks,
rape,
self-harm,
sexual assault,
therapy.

While some of these themes are only mentioned briefly, reader discretion is advised. Take care.

I would like to dedicate this book to my Nan, Lesley, who sadly passed in 2024. Thank you for showing me how to be a strong, independent, and ambitious woman.

Chapter 1

I am still in disbelief that my life has somehow become this good. For as long as I can remember, I've been drawn to the wrong type of guy, the ones who promised the world, only to chip away at my sense of self until I was little more than a reflection of their desires. Time and again, I let them mould me into their version of 'perfection', never realising how much of myself I was losing in the process. I suppose I am partially responsible, instead of going to therapy and working on myself, I just continued to let myself get into these situations. I was ignorant, never once considering the devastating toll these relationships would take on me as a woman. I carelessly dived headfirst into each new relationship, my naïve heart disregarding the inevitable pain and anguish that would follow. The weight of their aftermath threatened to crush my very being, scars that would linger long after the initial sting had faded. I have single-handedly allowed myself to be mistreated, but I clung to the hope that one day, I might find someone who would cherish me like I was their everything. Tonight, for example, I get to spend the night with my closest friends and my dream man, Jack.

Jack and I have been together for six months now. He's someone who came into my life when I least expected it. Jack is the kind of man who showers me with small acts of kindness. He buys me flowers unprompted, walks me home when it's dark to ensure my safety, spends the day with me whenever I'm feeling unwell, and will hold me at night as I break down and release my emotions. His thoughtfulness and attentiveness are the things that drew me to him. He makes me believe that I can do anything, and it has been quite a while since I've experienced that type of feeling. Before I met him, I felt like I was constantly looking over my shoulder, waiting for something awful to happen. We have each endured enough heartbreaks over the years, and we have earned this happiness.

This evening, we're going to Jack's brother's house. My best friend Lily will be joining us. Her and Jack have met before, a few times, but this will be the first time she meets my other friends. It's important to me that she has a good relationship with them. If Jack and I are to go all the way, then there will be many occasions where they have to spend time together.

My long, thick, and incredibly frizzy auburn hair has been straightened to within an inch of its life. I've dedicated a lot of my prep time to my makeup, ensuring my eyeliner wings are sharp enough to slay someone, and I've got a mix of soft matte brown eyeshadows on my lids to make my ocean blue eyes stand out even more than they typically do. My blue eyes happen to be one of the few features I've inherited from my birth father, those, and my height. Luckily for me, I mostly take after my mum. I've wrapped up the look with my go-to red lipstick, Russian Red from MAC. The bold red contrasts sharply with my porcelain skin, but if Taylor Swift can rock it, then I can too.

Currently, the weather is unusually warm for autumn in England, which is why I have chosen to wear my sole playsuit for this evening's event. It has black and white, vertical stripes, with a racer neck. Due to my height, I have always had a hard time with things like playsuits and jumpsuits, no one and I repeat no one wants to walk around with a camel toe. I only own one pair of "going out" shoes; they are black suede, lace-up heels, with small cutouts. The heel is two inches high and chunky, so I have less chance of falling over. I have, however, lost my little toenails many times when wearing them. At the end of the day, they don't make my feet ache like other pairs do, so why change something that half works? I would rather have a missing toenail than a broken ankle.

Lily has also worn a playsuit tonight; hers is a beige linen, off-the-shoulder one, paired with some fresh white trainers. Lily and I are both tall, so when we get dressed to go out, we usually opt for low heels or skip heels altogether. Her long, mousy brown hair is straight as well, with minimal makeup on her face. Lily was blessed with the gift of natural beauty. Her skin is always radiant with a natural glow, and unlike me, she can also achieve a tan, giving her a naturally bronzed appearance. The only makeup she wears is a touch of mascara to enhance the length of her lashes that frame her blue-grey eyes.

We finish our shots and start walking the short journey to the others. Currently, it's not just hot it's also humid, and I'm concerned that the effort I put into straightening my hair will be undone by the time we arrive. If you're a fan of Friends, remember the moment when Monica was in Barbados? That's exactly how my natural hair behaves. Every woman in our family has inherited the same thick, curly chaos on their heads, and we all straighten it to the extreme.

"If they make me uncomfortable, then I am just going to go home. You know that, right?" Lily says beside me.

"Lil, if they make you uncomfortable, then we will both be leaving. You know that, right?" I shove her shoulder with my own.

"You better mean that."

"When have I ever lied to you, Lil?"

"I don't believe you've ever done that," she gazes off thoughtfully, "but maybe you're so skilled at it that no one can ever tell."

"Lily, I can hardly put a sentence together, let alone lie to someone, especially you."

We're nearly at Jack's brother's house when I take out my phone to send him a text. He suggested coming out to meet us to make it less overwhelming for Lily. I've been friends with her since our first day in upper school, which means we've managed to stay close for ten years with hardly any conflicts. We were both outcasts and faced bullying throughout much of our school years. This shared experience brought us together, and we've been inseparable ever since, except for the years she spent at university. We've shared laughter, tears, and everything in between. I can assure you, we've experienced it all.

"Hello." I glance up to meet the gaze of the man standing before me. Jack is tall, dark, and undeniably handsome, fitting the ideal type of nearly every woman. His short, chocolate brown hair is casually swept to one side. His eyes are so dark they nearly appear black, but when the sunlight hits them, you can see the various shades of brown within. If you were to ask me, he has the perfect physique, though I admit I might be a bit biased. Not too skinny, with muscles in all the right spots. He wears deep black jeans, even in this heat, paired with a Ralph Lauren shirt that clings to his arms as if it were tailored just for him. Only when he smiles do I realise that my jaw is on the floor and the little voice inside my head is screaming *Pull yourself together, Olivia.*

"Hey," I can sense the immediate flush rising up my neck and onto my cheeks, fortunately concealed beneath the layers of foundation I've applied. Despite the fact that we've been together for some time now, I still find myself amazed each time I see him and come to the realisation that this is the man I get to share my life with.

"You two are so cute!" Lily squeals from beside me.

Jack takes me into his arms, squeezing every bit of air out of my lungs. When I gaze up at him, I can't help but see the smile lighting up his face. It's the kind of smile that brightens his large eyes, a genuine smile that accentuates his dimples beautifully. Removing one hand from my lower back, he lifts it to cradle my chin between his thumb and finger as he kisses me. This kiss is perhaps the softest and most tender I've ever experienced in my life. In fact, most of the kisses I share with him feel this way. His soft, full lips barely brush against mine before he pulls back, and then that smile reappears.

"Nice to see you again, Lily," he nods to her whilst loosening his other arm from around my waist, "let's get you inside to meet everyone."

I finally manage to peel my eyes off the man in front of me in time to notice the anxious look appear on my friend's face. Both of us are very introverted, and stepping into a home filled with unfamiliar faces could be the most torturous experience I could subject my friend to. Yet, she will still go through with it, as we would do anything for one another.

"You'll be fine! If I love you, then they will love you too," I say to her.

Lily closes her eyes and takes in a deep, shaky breath before saying, "Ok. Ok, let's go."

Jack nods at me before twisting on his feet to walk back to the house. I grab Lily's hand, wrapping it in mine, a gesture to show her she is not alone, and then we follow him.

The house from the outside is your standard-built house. A small front garden full of freshly laid green turf, accompanied by a pathway on the left leading to the front door. Further left of the path lies a small tarmac driveway, sufficient for parking one car. The house is constructed from a variety of deep orange bricks, which are still too new to show any signs of wear. His brother pays an extortionate amount of rent for the size of this house. Each time we visit, I find myself asking him if it's truly worth the cost.

I grip Lily's hand firmly as Jack swings open the front door, and the sounds of my other friends spill out onto the street. We don't need to exchange words, we understand each other so deeply that a single glance reveals our thoughts. The look Lily casts my way is one that clearly asks, '*Do we have to?*' In response, I give her a look that conveys, '*If they make you uncomfortable, we can leave.*' That's the honest truth. Despite my love for everyone in this house, Lily will always be my priority. She's like a second sister to me. We entered each other's lives at a time when we both needed someone.

Taking a deep breath, I guide Lily into the house.

Chapter 2

The night spent with my friends exceeded all my expectations. The anxiety I had about Lily was completely unnecessary, she blended in perfectly, as if she were the final piece of the puzzle.

Daisy and Georgia embraced Lily, keeping her close throughout the night, even during her bathroom breaks. These girls have no concept of personal boundaries. I've been friends with Georgia for almost a year, and I got to know Daisy through her. Wherever one goes, the other is sure to follow. I see a lot of myself and Lily in this duo; they are like sisters, though not related by blood. Georgia has long, jet-black hair, which she sleeked back into a tight bun on top of her head. Her eyes are a vibrant green, resembling emeralds nestled in her eye sockets rather than ordinary eyeballs. Daisy is around the same height as me, towering over Georgia. Her hair is shoulder-length, platinum blonde, with hazel eyes. While Georgia chose a super short and snug mini dress that showcased her curves beautifully, Daisy went for a pair of loose-fitting, low-rise black jeans paired with a white baby tee.

I feel incredibly thankful to have both of them in my life. I first met Georgia during a night out. I was with one of my old friends, Kimberly. However, Kim chose to leave me halfway through the evening to reunite with her ex-boyfriend. They never did end up back together. Georgia noticed I was alone and pulled me over to join her and Jordan on the dance floor. Since that moment, our friendship has flourished. We've even taken a girls' trip to Amsterdam together. Georgia is the extrovert to my introvert, and when I would go back to our hotel room to rest, she would stay out all night making new friends and questionable choices.

Jack's brother, who is another one of my closest friends, Jordan, has had a crush on Georgia since the first time I met them both. However, neither of them is willing to express their feelings to one another, leaving the rest of us to endure the awkward tension whenever they share the same space. I was introduced to Jack by Jordan. One day, he came into my workplace to see if I wanted to join him at our local nightclub – if you can even call it that – and Jack was with him.

We got talking on that night out and bonded over our earlier heartbreaks and love for our family and friends. As Jordan knew us both well, he was happy for us to explore a relationship with each other, knowing we would be exactly what the other one needed. Jordan is a few years older than Jack and me. They share the same height and similar features, the genetics in that family are remarkably strong. However, Jordan spends a lot of time at the gym, resulting in a more toned and muscular physique.

Together we have shared drinks, danced side by side, and caught up on everything that has happened in our lives since our last night out, which was just last weekend. Us girls snapped countless selfies to share online while the boys engaged in discussions about their family issues. When we all get together, it feels like a second family, perhaps a bit more chaotic than our biological families, but a family built on friendships that will last for a lifetime.

Jack and I have said goodbye to our friends. Georgia and Daisy are heading home together since they live on the same street, while Lily has hopped into a taxi as she lives just outside the town. Now, we only have a brief walk across town to get back to my house.

Since earlier the weather has thankfully cooled down significantly. It’s still humid, yet my hair has managed to survive the night. It’s also warm enough to not feel the cold, but that could be because of the endless cups of pink gin and lemonade consumed. Regardless, Jack drapes his jacket over my shoulders because he wants to make sure I don't get cold. Ever since we first met, he has always taken care of me.

With my hand in his, Jack exhales deeply, saying, "That wasn't too terrible, was it?"

“No,” I let out a small chuckle. “No, it wasn’t. I was so worried for Lily, but she fit right in. I don’t think Georgia even let her go to the toilet on her own.”

“That’s our Georgia for you, no sense of personal space.”

"We wouldn't want her to be any different. It was lovely to spend the evening together, and for a change, there was no drama."

"You realise it's always Georgia and Jordan who stir up the trouble, right?" He nudges my shoulder. "But don't tempt fate," Jack laughs. "We're not back home yet, there's still a chance for something to go horribly wrong."

Home. I already feel like I am home. This man feels like home to me. Growing up, I didn’t have a man that made me feel safe. That’s how dads are supposed to make you feel, right? Instead, when it was Richard’s weekend to see me and my sister Rose, he would take us to the local pub in the village where he used to live. He would leave us at a table alone in the corner with a bag of crisps and a can of Coke, while he went off to get drunk with his friends. We would spend hours just sitting there in the corner of the shabby pub, surrounded by unfamiliar drunk men, until it was time for him to take us back to Nan’s house, where Mum would pick us up. At that time, we were five and eight years old, and I felt anything but safe. However, the courts were indifferent to our feelings. They told our mum that we were too young to know what we wanted. The last time I heard from him was when he sent me a Facebook friend request a decade ago, without any accompanying message. I ultimately rejected it because he had missed out on so much of my life, and I refuse to let him use my social media to update his friends and portray himself as a good father.

We walk the rest of the way home in silence. Usually, silence makes me feel awkward, and I will do anything in my power to fill it, but with Jack, it’s different. There’s contentment in the silence. I still live at home with my mum, I’m hoping to save my money up to buy a house of my own one day, or even a house for me and Jack when the time is right. My ideal scenario would be to have a detached house, complete with a garage and driveway, and enough land so I could own a horse. I am fully aware that the chances of this becoming a reality are slim, but a girl can dream.

Carefully and as quietly as possible, I unlock the front door, fully conscious that even the faintest sound could wake our family dog up. Once we are inside, I lock the door behind us, somehow managing not to wake the beast with supersonic hearing. Our next task to tackle is the world's squeakiest staircase. When I'm sober, I know which steps to steer clear of, but after a few drinks… that's a whole different ballgame. I'm certain that whenever you attempt to be as stealthy as possible, you inevitably end up creating the loudest racket imaginable. Laughing together like the grown-ups we are, we finally reach the top, and fortunately for us, my room is the first one right off the staircase.

I quickly prepare for bed by removing my makeup and gathering my hair into a messy bun. I usually adhere to a strict skincare regimen that I try to follow as often as possible, as it helps control my eczema. However, tonight, all I can manage is applying the moisturiser. This is perhaps the most challenging aspect of living with chronic illnesses; there's only so much you can accomplish in a day before the exhaustion and chronic fatigue take over. I sleep in one of Jack's T-shirts, which reaches the top of my thigh. While they are indeed comfortable, the real reason I wear them is because they smell of his incredible aftershave. As I lie in bed, I rest my head on my man's chest, drape one of my legs over his, and then I'm hit with the sudden realisation that I need to get up for work in just five hours.

"Do you think that if I call in sick tomorrow, they'll realise I've been out tonight?" I inquire into the shadows.

Jack laughs, saying, "I believe that they will fall apart if you don't go in. Close your eyes and get some rest."

"Don't laugh at me, you get to go home and go back to sleep."

"If you want to call in sick, then that decision is yours to make. You know I won't complain about spending more time with you."

"You could just come to work with me. We could hide you in the staff room, no one would ever know."

"You think they wouldn't notice you missing from the shop floor?"

"You make a good point there." I let out a big sigh. "I hate it when you're right."

He tucks a strand of escaped hair behind my ear and places a kiss on the crown of my head. "Sleep, Olivia."

The worlds biggest yawn escapes me, and I close my eyes. I think about the events of tonight, how lucky I am to have such incredible friends. It makes me so happy knowing that we can do stuff all together now. They loved Lily! At the end of the night, it was like she had been part of our little group the entire time.

The final thought on my mind, before the darkness takes over and I fall into a deep sleep is how happy I am. After a life of one terrible thing after another, I am genuinely happy, and it's all because of the man whose arms I am sleeping in tonight.

Chapter 3

After seven hours of hell, I have one hour left of my shift. Normally, I love being here, but today, all I'm craving is my bed. My head feels as if someone has smashed it with a hammer, and then ran over it with a car, and no amount of paracetamol and caffeine in the world can make it tolerable. Pink gin may taste like juice, but juice never leaves me feeling this awful. I keep telling myself that I'll never go out drinking again, but deep down, I know that's a lie. Hangovers used to be so much easier to handle when I was eighteen, now it takes nearly three days to shift it.

I work as an assistant manager at E.O newsagents, the sole newsagents in our town since the others have closed. I believe the main reason this one continues to operate is because it belongs to a large corporate chain, which gives them more financial resources than their smaller competitors.

Honestly, I have put in an unbelievable amount of effort to get where I am today. I began my journey here with morning shifts while I was preparing for my A-levels. At first, balancing work and study didn't seem too challenging. However, when exam time arrived, I faced significant difficulties and ended up failing. After deciding not to retake the exams, I increased my hours at work. I would arrive early to organize and display the new newspapers and magazines before the store opened. One of the girls who bullied me in middle school was my superior with the position of key holder. It was a mix of both humiliation and empowerment. I felt immense pride in showing up for work every day and sharing the same space with her after everything she had put me through.

The bullying began in primary school when they would hide my lunchbox and fill my water bottle with soapy water, forcing me to drink it. By middle school, the harassment escalated to name-calling, pushing, shoving, and cyberbullying. For me the cyberbullying was the worst, she would send such vile messages to me telling me to end my life. It might not seem like much as an adult but as a nine-year-old, it was the worst thing in the world to read. I used to be a confident little girl, but they stripped that away, leaving me a vulnerable and anxious wreck.

When the assistant manager position opened up, we both applied for it. Ultimately, I was the one who got the job, and shortly after, she resigned. She claimed it was due to a 'better opportunity,' yet she remained unemployed four months later. *A small victory for Olivia White.*

There are a lot of things I love about my job, from the people I work with, to the regular daily customers who come in to get their newspapers. Some of the older customers stay a little while to update you on their lives and to get updates on yours. I sometimes wonder if we are the only people they'll get to talk to that day, so I always make sure I have time for them. What I love most about my job is undoubtedly the books. There are endless shelves filled with nonfiction, fiction, and children's literature. Whatever you can think of, we have it.

As kids, Rose and I had a floor to ceiling bookshelf that was packed with books. For a while, I was particularly fond of Michael Morpurgo's stories. I've been passionate about reading for as long as I can remember. The ability to escape reality was something I craved during my childhood, and now, I can't imagine anything more delightful than snuggling up with a steamy Elsie Silver novel and a cup of tea after a long, tiring day.

Today has been manic. I've rearranged half of the shop, moving our fiction books from one wall to another. They're still down the same aisle, so I don't see what the big change was for, but the head office has decided it's necessary. Apparently, it will "boost our sales by forty percent." To be frank, the only way we could significantly increase our sales is by not pricing our products extortionately, especially when you can find the same items on Amazon for half the cost. All I have left to do today is finish restocking this week's bestseller chart. Jade – my new key holder since the last one resigned – comes out from behind the till to help me.

“You look how I feel!” She remarks, scanning me from head to toe, attempting to conceal her grin but not quite succeeding.

“Don’t even start. I think I managed to get just over four hours of sleep last night.”

She picks up a pile of books and starts restocking the shelves. “You know, he shouldn’t keep you up that late when you have work the next day.”

“Oh, my goodness, Jade! It was nothing like that.”

“I’m just saying,” she holds her hands up in defence. “You work hard here. You don’t need to be coming in tired and ruining everything that you have worked so hard for.”

“I’m not going to ruin anything. I’m still here, aren’t I?” I wave in her face. “Besides, would you get eight hours of sleep every night if you were laid next to him?”

“I get ten hours every night because I choose not to have a man keep me up.”

“I usually get at least seven,” I mumble under my breath.

She turns to me with one eyebrow raised like she doesn’t believe me before turning back around to finish what she was doing. Jade has worked here for a little over a year now, and she has become another good friend of mine. Though she’s a good five years younger than me, at the ripe age of eighteen, she’s more mature than a lot of people my age.

She has thin, shoulder-length hair that she has dyed so many times I have lost count. The ends are now so dry and frazzled that the only way to save her hair would be to cut it all off and start again. At the moment, it’s a deep purple, her eyes are hazel, more of a gold than they are brown, and of course, she’s wearing her signature winged eyeliner. Jade seems to be the only person I know who has the energy for a complete makeup look on a Sunday morning. I do remember being her age though and never stepping out without my makeup applied and my hair styled. The years of abuse from various people left me feeling so insecure with who I was. However, since being with Jack, I've ventured out without any makeup, and I no longer feel the need to hide my natural appearance. He assures me that I'm beautiful just as I am, and I trust him because he truly makes me feel that way.

The rest of the hour goes by quickly, thank goodness, and we quickly close the shop up together. When she started working here, we realised she only lived around the corner from me, so we walk the short walk home from work together. Tonight, though, as we turn to start our ten-minute journey home, I find Jack standing there waiting for me.

He is so incredibly handsome, even in a pair of skinny, over-washed, black jogging bottoms. His matching hoody is oversized. He wears his hood up to hide his messy, freshly washed hair.

"Hey, I thought you were meeting Jordan tonight?" I ask because he didn't mention he was walking me home. In fact, I'm not sure he has ever walked me home from work before. He walks me home in the dark, yes, but never from work when it's still light outside, and I have someone to walk with.

"I was meant to be," he says whilst pulling me to his chest, "but some things are more important."

I let out a soft giggle and glance at Jade, who has begun to walk backwards as if she can't escape us fast enough. She has always had this reaction when it comes to Jack. I'm still trying to decide if she secretly hates him for some reason or if she has a little crush.

"I'll see you tomorrow!" She blurts out before turning around and speeding off down the street.

My brows pull together slightly but I take Jack's hand in mine and start the walk home. In this relationship, I'm really putting in the effort to let go of all the hurt that previous boyfriends have caused me, to prevent myself from overanalysing every little detail in this one. It's silent for a while, yet again a content silence that doesn't need filling. Jack is the first to speak.

"What's your favourite flower?"

The question throws me off right away since this man has gifted me numerous bouquets over the past six months. “If I had to pick, I would have to say tulips. I like all flowers, but I do have a soft spot for tulips. They’re just a little bit different, aren’t they? Not everyone thinks about tulips. Why?”

He stops abruptly, causing me to almost lose my footing as my arm is pulled back. I glance at him, seeing a blend of anger and perhaps a hint of sadness in his eyes. “So, you’ve let me buy you flowers you don’t even like since we’ve been together?”

I find myself somewhat surprised by the tone of his voice and the fierce intensity in his gaze. It's certainly not sadness, there's only anger reflected in his eyes. “No, that isn’t what I said. I said I like all flowers, but you asked what my favourite was.”

“I have never given you tulips, Olivia. How am I supposed to know these things unless you tell me? I have wasted so much money on flowers you don’t even want.”

I've never witnessed this side of Jack. He's never shouted at me. Me being me, I attempt to ease the tension a bit, as I really dislike any form of conflict. “It isn’t a waste of money, Jack. I love every single bunch you buy me. I just told you what my favourite is because you asked. You’ve never asked me before. Now you know for next time,” I finish off with a wink.

What a mistake that was. His nostrils start to flare, and his breathing becomes shallow and irregular. He releases my hand and shakes his head at me before angrily walking away down the street. A wave of panic washes over me. I never intended to upset him, that’s the last thing I would want. I imagine he’s probably having a difficult day, so I decide to backtrack on what I’ve said in the hope of making his day slightly better.

“Maybe I’m wrong!” I shout after him. This makes him stop and turn back towards me. “Roses are better.”

He hangs his head, and a smile appears on his face. He runs his hand through his hair under his hood. Walking back towards me, he holds his hand out for me to take, saying, "I don't want to fight with you, Olivia, but when you say stuff like that, it makes me feel like I'm doing the wrong thing."

"Of course not. I'm sorry, it's my fault," I say, reaching up to peck him on the cheek.

The rest of the walk home is silent, but it is no longer a happy silence. It's a silence full of tension. *What on earth was that?* The man asked what my favourite flower was, and I told him. Why ask the question if you don't want to know the answer?

We say goodbye, and he leaves to meet Jordan at the gym. He seems to think that exercise is a good way to burn his massive hangover off. Maybe he's right, maybe it is the hangover causing his erratic mood swings.

"Is he not coming in?" Mum asks from the kitchen.

My mum, my incredible mum. Harriet White is a pocket rocket. She's the most extraordinary woman I have ever met in my life. She raised Rose and I by herself. At one point, she was working three different jobs to provide for us. These, of course, worked around our busy school and gymnastics schedules. She did everything she could for us growing up. She is my biggest inspiration in life. I can't imagine it was easy being a single mum with two children. No matter how much she struggled with money, she always made sure we never went without anything.

She shares my auburn hair colour. Hers is styled in a chin-length bob with a fringe. Her skin tone might be slightly darker than mine, though that could be due to the freckles sprinkled across her entire body. Her eyes are a mixture of grey and green, but if you asked her, she would describe them as a hue of "pond water." She stands a good four inches shorter than I do, yet she still towers over Rose and measures every quarter of an inch.

"No, not today. He's already late for meeting Jordan, so he had to run," I say to her, walking through to the kitchen.

Our kitchen is a spacious open layout, with three of the four walls painted in a soft magnolia, while the fourth wall is covered with a rich red floral wallpaper. The flooring consists of slate grey tiles that beautifully complement the white cabinets and countertops. One wall is lined with white cupboards, and there is plenty of room for a table that can seat six people comfortably.

My mum finishes wiping down the sides and looks at me with a massive grin on her face. "His brother lives at that gym, doesn't he? You've got a good one, you know. He really cares about his family."

I'm still shocked by what just happened, and I can't bring myself to tell my mum about it. It's probably me overthinking and being silly. I'm sure he will be back to his usual bubbly self tomorrow. He does wear his heart on his sleeve and cares for those around him so deeply, that he puts their needs before his own. So, I change the topic of the conversation completely to "Where's Dad?"

Now, this is going to confuse a lot of people. As I said, my mum raised Rose and I by herself. She did. She met my dad when I was twelve and Rose was fifteen. He stayed the night and just never really left. He moved in properly after six months. When I say properly, I mean he just moved the stuff he had not used in the last six months from my grandma's house to our house. I gave him a tough time for the first year they were together, testing him to see if he was good enough for my mum. I used to live with the opinion that no one was good enough for her. She deserved the world in my eyes, and no man alive could give that to her. It turns out he is an incredible man who loves everything about her. He makes her happier than I have ever seen her, and she deserves that. I actually can't remember my mum having any boyfriends when we were growing up, so I should have known when we were finally allowed to meet him that he was a good one.

When he would come over, she used to send us upstairs to our rooms, and we were not allowed back down until he was gone. I know now it was her way of keeping us safe in case he wasn't the man she thought he was. I remember the night we were allowed to meet him like it was yesterday. He bought a DVD for us to watch together. It was the first Avatar movie, none of us had watched either of the films before that night, but Rose got a migraine after an hour and had to go to bed. He wasn't put off by it, and we managed to watch the film the next time he came over. When I was seventeen, after many conversations with my mum, we sat around the table, and I asked him if he would adopt me. Lee White being the incredible, selfless man he is, accepted. The conversation ended with all of us in tears, but I now have a dad I can be proud of. A man who took on two teenage girls as his own and never looked back.

"Oh, he's at football right now. He will be back for dinner, though."

"Your husband lives on the football pitch, doesn't he?" I throw her a wink as I shove her shoulder.

"He's either there or he is off on one of his many golfing adventures," she gives me an over-exaggerated eye roll.

"Oh, don't forget about darts as well," we laugh at each other.

My dad loves sport. He has played football since he was a child. In our eyes he's the best goalkeeper around, but he's also the best golfer and best darts player as well. I have no idea how he manages it all alongside a full-time job and his family. But he does.

With that I start helping my mum prepare dinner. Dinner at the Whites is not for the faint-hearted. Any opportunity my dad or I get to stir the pot with some wildly inappropriate dinner chatter, we seize it! I wouldn't have it any other way. When Rose joins us for dinner, it gets even crazier. My mum usually finds herself at the end of the table, head in hands, mumbling a desperate plea for someone to rescue her from the circus she calls home. She puts on her best annoyed face, but that smile of hers sneaks out before long.

Chapter 4

The next few weeks go by in a blur. It has been a mixture of working and spending time with my family and Jack. I haven't had a chance to see Lily, Georgia, or Daisy, but they all check in via text to make sure I'm still alive. Jack continues to buy me more roses just as the others start to die. They do brighten up my otherwise boring bedroom.

I now occupy the second largest room since Rose has moved out. There is plenty of space for a black metal double bed and a small, very old brown leather sofa that is beginning to peel, yet I'm determined not to throw it out. There's a black wardrobe, a bedside table and a matching set of drawers. The walls are painted magnolia – everything in this house is magnolia – with one wall featuring black floral designed wallpaper. I decided that having carpet in my room was too risky, it would inevitably be stained by various makeup products, so I opted for deep grey laminate flooring instead, complemented by a black shaggy rug beside my bed. The laminate is much easier to maintain but is absolutely freezing in the mornings. The red roses certainly bring a splash of colour to the room.

After walking me home, Jack sits himself down on my sofa and starts scrolling through his phone whilst I grab the things I need for a shower after work. Just as I set my things down in the bathroom and turn the shower on, my phone goes off. I dry my hands off with my towel and pick it up. The name flashing on the screen is one I never wanted to encounter in my life. Bile surges up my throat, accompanied by its close friend, anxiety. With trembling fingers, I unlock my phone to read the message from Jack's ex, Katie.

Katie: Hi, just thought I would let you know your "boyfriend" is still telling me he loves me and wants me back. If you could kindly tell him to leave me alone, that would be great, thanks.

Instantly, my anxiety increases leaving me to feel more nauseous than I already did. The bile makes my mouth slick with saliva. *Is this why he has been off with me? Is this why we suddenly keep having small arguments? He doesn't want to be with me.*

That doesn't make any sense, though. Surely, he would just leave me if he didn't want to be with me? He has just started spending more time with me. Surely, if he didn't want to be here, then he wouldn't be. I lock my phone again and get into the shower. I slide down until I am sitting, letting the water wash over me and block out the sound of my cries.

With everything I have endured, I can't help but think the worst. The paranoia consumes me. I wish I could escape it, yet this is the reality of my mind now. Whenever I am happy, my brain will sabotage that happiness until there is nothing but dark depression left. Two of my earlier boyfriends have been unfaithful to me. One went as far as sleeping with another girl. The other was messaging multiple women behind my back. Both of those things leave scars.

I'm not sure how long I've been sitting here. It could be minutes or even hours. Panic attacks are the norm for me now. The water is starting to run cold, so I know it's time to get out. Once I'm dried and dressed in my usual leggings and oversized T-shirt, I wrap my hair up in a towel on top of my head. Taking a deep breath, I unlock the bathroom door and walk down the small landing back to my bedroom, where Jack is still sitting, scrolling.

"What are you even looking at on there?" I ask as I dig around under my bed for my hairdryer, not sure how to bring the conversation up.

"Nothing." He says bluntly without looking up.

"Can we talk?"

"We are talking."

Ok. That's how it's going to be then.

My hope that things would get better again was short-lived because since that day he asked me what my favourite flower was, I feel like everything I do or say seems to upset him in some way. It wasn't the hangover after all. I take my phone out of my bra and screenshot the message from Katie and send it to him, knowing this is the only way I am going to get his attention. I sit myself down on the edge of my bed and watch him, waiting for him to open the message.

Jack's face pales as he opens the message. "What the fuck is this?" He asks. He finally takes his eyes off his phone to look up at me. *Is that panic on his face? Is she telling the truth?*

"I don't know, Jack. Why don't you tell me?"

"She's just trying to get in your head. Ignore her."

"Is she?" I ask carefully. I know better than to poke the bear, but I deserve answers. "We have argued a lot recently. Is this why?"

If looks could kill, I would be dead, even more than dead if that's possible. He locks his phone and throws it on the sofa, pulling himself forward so he is sitting on the very edge. "No, Olivia. We have argued because you don't recognise all I do for you," he says with such a condescending tone.

"That…That's not true, Jack." My brows pull together. "I appreciate everything you do for me. You know that's not true. Why would she say it if it didn't happen?" I ask, trying and failing to keep my voice steady.

"This is you all over, Olivia!" His voice grows louder with each word. "Just because you have trust issues doesn't give you the right to assume the worst of me!"

He is right. I do have trust issues, but only because every man who has been in my life, other than my dad, has caused me pain or betrayal. Whether that has been from abandonment or them being unfaithful, I have been hurt far too many times to keep count. I know he's different from the people I've been with before, none of them have cared for me the way that Jack does. What I can't grasp is why he is reacting so defensively. Why his face is a picture of panic? Or is that just my paranoia resurfacing once more?

I stand and walk over to where he is sitting and kneel in front of him. I hold his hands in mine, look him in the eye, and ask him what I have been wanting to ask him for weeks now but haven't had the right moment to do so. "I need to know, Jack. I need to know if I'm not enough for you."

What happens next, happens so fast I barely have time to register it before it's happened. Jack stands, snatching his hands away from me and knocking me over in the process. I bang my head against the edge of the bed frame. The towel does nothing to soften the impact. He runs his hands through his hair while yelling, "why are you still making this about you? You're giving her exactly what she wants by doubting me. Do you really think I would waste all my time with you if I didn't want to be with you? How do you think you're making me feel right now?"

Holding the back of my head with one hand, trying to register what the hell is going on, I notice I have started to cry again. *Great.* The tears just keep coming. "I'm not trying to make you feel anything, Jack. I don't want to argue with you. I am just trying to understand why Katie would reach out if there's nothing going on. She has had months to try and come between us. Why now?"

"Why are you making this into something it's not? It's just a message from a girl who has too much time on her hands."

"Well, you won't mind if I go on your phone and check then, will you?" I say, but I dare not move. I'm testing him. *So much for not wanting to poke the bear.*

"Touch my phone, Olivia, and I swear I'll storm out of this damn house right now, and you'll never lay eyes on me again!" His face is a shade of crimson by the time he finishes his explosive outburst. He strides a few steps, then punches the wall with his fist. "FUCK."

I sit paralysed in terror for what feels like an eternity. Time seems to stand still. This is the man who has held me close during my darkest nights, soothing me through the memories of my turbulent childhood. He's the one who cradled me while I wept uncontrollably, a man with a heart so big and who cares so deeply for those he loves. He's not someone who erupts like this.

He holds his right hand to his chest as he lowers himself back onto the sofa, placing his head in his free hand. I get up then and go to him, before assessing his hand to make sure he hasn't done too much damage. The wall is intact, so that tells me his hand lost this fight. *Why would anyone punch a brick wall?* His knuckles are already bruising, and swelling, and a few small cuts are bleeding on two of his knuckles. I take his head in my hands and look him in the eye as I say, "you're right. I'm sorry. You wouldn't do that to me. To us. Let's forget about it."

"I wouldn't do this to you, Olivia. I know what it's like. I would not do that to you." He is right…again. He does know what it's like. When he and Katie broke up, he learnt she had been cheating on him for eighteen months. Someone who knows what that feels like would never inflict that sort of hurt on someone else.

"Wait here. I will get you some peas to put on your hand." I leave the room without looking back. I'm not even sure if he responds to me because suddenly, I'm hit with a flashback.

They still come often even though I haven't seen Richard since I was seven years old. Him and Jack aren't the same, though, are they? It *is* my fault. I pushed him too far. He would never hurt me. *Would he?*

Whilst downstairs I take a few minutes to myself, leaning against the kitchen counter for balance, focusing on my breathing to try and push the rising panic aside. I'm not entirely sure why I said I was sorry because I'm not. It's normal to want answers and reassurance from your partner when something like this happens. I have never seen him get that angry before, and it terrified me. For the first time since we have been together, *he* has frightened me. I thought he was different from the rest. *No. He is.* This was just because I pushed him too far. I know he doesn't like to talk about Katie. It will not happen again.

I push myself from the side and rummage in the freezer until I find the bag of forgotten peas from the very bottom. I wrap them in a tea towel and make my way back upstairs. Jack is still sitting on the sofa, now holding his right hand in his left.

"Here," I say as I pass him the wrapped-up peas. "You can't get angry like that, Jack. I will not sit back and put up with that kind of behaviour."

"You pushed me, Olivia. Was I meant to just sit back and take a verbal beating from you?" He puts the pea parcel on his knee and lowers his right hand on top of it.

"I was just asking. You would do the same if you got that message from one of my exes."

"No, I wouldn't." His dark eyes find mine. "That is where we are different. I would never think so lowly of you. She has messaged me a few times, yes, but I've ignored her."

"Why didn't you just tell me that? All you had to do was tell me the truth, and I would have dropped it, Jack. I will not put up with you punching things because you're frustrated. I cannot and will not allow myself to go through this stuff again."

He nods and presses his forehead against mine.

That's why she did it, then? Because he wasn't giving her the attention she wanted.

A little while later, Jack and I are sat opposite each other at the kitchen table. It's Friday night, which means it's a takeaway night in the White household. My mum is rushing around getting plates and cutlery ready when my dad bursts through the door. "Grubs up, people."

My dad has a head of deep brown hair, the same colour as Jack's. It's short on the sides and longer on the top. His jaw is peppered with a small amount of stubble. He has your typical dad body with a slight beer belly, but he has incredibly toned legs from his years of football. He towers over all of us.

Me and Jack have not spoken since earlier. Both of us have sat here in silence. We moved from my room to the kitchen when the initial pain started to wear off, and the peas started to defrost. If I'm being totally honest, I am still frightened to say the wrong thing and set him off again. He has always been so good to me, taking me out for fancy dinners, buying me flowers, walking me home from work, buying me gifts just because, holding me when the nightmares wake me up. Today has really thrown me, though I do suppose everyone has a breaking point. The swelling on his hand has gone down since earlier. The only proof of what happened are the bruises still forming on his knuckles and the small cuts that are only visible up close. He has his hand hidden from my parents in the pocket on the front of his hoody.

"You two are awfully quiet," my mum says as she joins us at the table. What do I say to her? Do I tell her the truth? Would she even believe me? Would she tell me I'm overreacting and overthinking?

Luckily for me, Jack jumps in before I get the chance to respond. "Olivia had an exhausting day at work, didn't you, babe?" He says whilst looking at me dead in the eye from across the table as if to say, *"don't you dare tell them what happened."*

"Yeah, our delivery was wrong, and it's messed us up for next week," I reply, going along with his lie. There was nothing wrong with my delivery. In fact, the delivery came yesterday, not today.

"Don't you be taking it out on the poor boy. Leave work at work. It's not worth bringing it home with you." My mum says whilst rummaging through the bags of food to start serving it up.

I look away from Jack and turn my gaze to my mum. Honestly, she's the most stunning woman I've ever laid eyes on. Even in her early fifties, she has such a beautiful glow about her. I can't tell her what happened. It could break her heart to know how he acted if she even believed me. She doesn't want me and Rose to go through the same things she had to. Also, if she believed me, she would tell my dad, and they would both drag him out of the house and wouldn't let him step inside ever again. If it was just a one-off, is it even worth bringing up? I decide to keep it to myself for now. So, I simply give her a small smile and help her with the bags instead.

After we have all finished eating, I help my mum scrape the leftovers into the bin and load the dirty dishes into the dishwasher, whilst Jack and my dad go and sit in the living room to talk football.

"Are you ok, baby? You still seem off?" Mum asks whilst tucking a loose strand of hair behind my ear. This woman knows me like the back of her hand. I have never been able to hide anything from her. In fact, I've never tried. I watched Rose try to lie to her for years as a teenager, and she saw through every single one. Call it a mother's intuition.

"Yeah, I'm all good, just a rough day at work, that's all. I just need a good night's sleep, and I am sure I will feel better in the morning!" I say to her once I've finished adding the last plate into the dishwasher. I haven't technically lied, I believe tomorrow is a new day and everything will return to normal.

She pulls me in close, enveloping me in her arms. Being taller than her does have its benefits because I am able to bend my neck slightly and rest my chin on her shoulder. A long sigh escapes me, one I didn't even realise I was holding. Tears threaten to leak from my eyes again, but I blink them back and let her go, giving her a peck on the cheek as I turn to walk into the living room to join the others.

Our living room is rather spacious. There really is no other way to put it. With beach wood-coloured flooring, the standard magnolia on three of the four walls and a feature wall of flowered wallpaper that are various shades of green. Most rooms in this house share a similar décor style, which is very feminine as it always has been in any house we've lived in. My dad knows he's outnumbered, so he never tries to fight us when it comes to painting and decorating, and I know deep down he secretly loves it. We have a large corner sofa, made of brown leather like the one in my room, although this one doesn't have leather peeling from it. It's covered in an assortment of little cushions all a different shade of green, to match the colours on the wallpaper.

My dad is in his usual spot in the corner of the sofa with his feet up on the matching ottoman and our family dog, Roger, curled up at his side. Jack is sitting on the left end of the sofa, right by the kitchen door. My mum sits on the far right of the sofa, leaving me with the choice to either sit between my mum and dad, or between Jack and my dad.

I stand there for a second, thinking about whether I sit next to Jack and pretend nothing has happened or sit between my parents and risk being asked questions. Before I make my decision, Jack reaches up and grabs my hand. I start to sit down beside him, but he pulls me onto his lap. I sit across his lap, and he pulls my head into his chest. He holds me there for a few moments before kissing the crown of my head.

"Thank you," he whispers into my hair. The TV volume is so high no one else can hear him. "I am so sorry, Olivia, it will not happen again. I am so sorry."

I relax further into him and then lift my head slightly to look into his eyes. There's no anger in them anymore, only the warmth that I usually see when I look into them, the same eyes I fell in love with. "I'm sorry, too. I shouldn't have pushed you," I say before leaning in to give him a quick peck on the lips.

This moment tells me I was right earlier. I didn't need to worry my mum and dad with what happened. It was a one-off. He knows what he did was wrong, and it won't happen again.

We spend the rest of the evening watching Friday night TV with my parents. When my dad is home, he's in charge of the TV, so it was an evening spent watching reruns of Traffic Cops, which makes a difference to the usual football matches we have to watch. The events of earlier today are a distant memory when we excuse ourselves to go up to bed.

Now lying in bed, in our usual position, my head on his chest with one leg thrown over his, Jack strokes my hair, and I feel safe again. There is something so calming about the way he holds me. I forget about everything else, and my attention is completely on him. I'm almost falling asleep when he speaks, making me jump.

"I can't wait to marry you one day, you know?"

I turn my head slightly to look up at him. My room is so dark I can't really see anything other than a rough outline of his head.

“Really?” I ask. “It would be one hell of a party, wouldn’t it?”

He chuckles, “Yeah, it would. I can imagine you walking down the aisle in a big, puffy white dress. Your hair in that braided up-do you know I like. You would take everyone's breath away. You really are so beautiful, Olivia.”

“You would look amazing in a suit,” a small laugh leaves me. “It’s something I have tried to picture many times now.”

“Well, one day, you won’t have to use your imagination.”

“You would really marry me?”

“Of course, I’ve always wanted to get married.” He pauses, stroking my hair to think. “I would run away and do it right now if I thought our mothers wouldn’t kill us.”

“Even if they didn’t murder us for not inviting them, it is a little too soon for that, isn’t it? We are still learning things about each other.”

“No Liv. The promise of a lifetime full of making memories with you could never be too soon. I can’t wait to make you mine.”

He reaches down then to kiss me passionately. Claiming me as his own like he does every other night.

Chapter 5

I left for work early this morning, giving me time to pop into the coffee shop and pick up drinks for both myself and Jade before the Saturday morning rush begins. Jack walked down with me on his way home to shower before going out with Jordan for breakfast. I must come into this shop at least twice a day for my fix of caffeine, and in the winter, the occasional hot chocolate. In fact, it doesn't matter if it's me who goes in or whether it's Jade, they instinctively know our order and start preparing it the second we walk through the door. Some would argue it's because we're in there so often, but I believe it's due to the staff's incredible ability to remember everyone's drink preferences. My sister's boyfriend, Rob, is the manager here, but today he has an odd day off. They have been together for a few years now and are looking forward to welcoming their first baby.

With the two drinks in my hand, one iced caramel latte for me and one hot chocolate for Jade, I walk through the shop to the staff room, where I find her waiting. I'm fairly confident she is the only person who works here that manages to make the uniform look trendy. She has the navy-blue shirt tucked into her worn black skinny jeans, paired with some black vans.

"How did I manage to beat you? You're usually here before me," she says, not looking up from her phone.

I clear my throat, and she glances up. "Oh, my goodness, you're a lifesaver! Did they give me extra cream?" She inquires as she springs up to grab her hot chocolate from me.

"I imagine so. They usually do. I will get you to try coffee one day. You'll be left wondering how you ever managed to live life without it."

"I'll just keep my Redbull, thank you very much."

"That stuff is like a slow poison, Jade. It will kill you."

"I'm here for a good time, not a long time," she winks at me.

"You really are a walking ick," I wink back at her.

"Don't tell me you haven't craved an ice cold Redbull on a hot summers day?"

"Obviously, I have. That still doesn't make it good for you."

We sit there for a while, drinking our drinks before we go onto the shop floor to prepare for the day ahead. After the newspapers are filled with their accompanying Saturday magazines, and the shelves are replenished and ready to go, we open for the day. Our first customer is the same no matter what the day or weather. An elderly lady with short silver hair. She always wears a long-pleated skirt, a pair of skin-coloured tights, with a short-sleeved T-shirt tucked in. The typical outfit your nan might wear. In the time I have worked here I've learnt a lot about her life. Her name is Sheila, she has one sister, a few years younger than her, she is a widow and has been for over ten years, and she has no children, which was not her choice, but she just failed to conceive.

"There're my favourite girls. How are you both today?" Sheila asks as she approaches the till with her battered shopping trolley in one hand and a newspaper in the other.

"Morning, Sheila," we both say in unison.

"I'm happy it's a little cooler today, they've turned the air conditioning off now, preparing for winter, so hopefully it won't be too hot in here today." I say as I take her paper from her to scan it through the till. "How about you, how are you today?"

"Oh, you know me dear. Nothing new. I am supposed to go to and see my sister this afternoon and stay for the week, but her car broke down, and now I don't know if she will be able to get me."

"Could you get the bus there?" Jade asks, carefully putting her newspaper into a small bag so it doesn't get damaged in her trolley whilst she does the rest of her shopping in town.

One thing I don't think I will ever understand is how older people go to town daily. There's always something they need. I do know Sheila goes for breakfast with a few of her friends every morning to get out and socialise, but we see her walking up and down the High Street for hours afterward.

"I could do… it'll just mean I have to take all my bags with me," her aged hands shake as she hands me the money for her paper.

"Well," I say as I hand her the change. "Hopefully, she can get her car fixed this morning."

"I hope so, dear. You girls look after yourselves. I want to hear everything when I get back."

I let out a small chuckle and walk to the door to hold it open as she leaves, leaving Jade to serve the next customer.

"Have a great time, Sheila. We'll see you when you get home."

The next two hours pass by quickly. Jade and I have been rushed off our feet. It's more hectic than usual as some parents are busy getting a head start on their Christmas shopping. It's only October, but from the few years I've worked here, I have learnt that parents like to be prepared. I hope that if I am fortunate enough to become a mother someday, I too will be organised. Maggie, our weekend staff member, has come in to take over at the register, allowing Jade and me to begin labelling a large selection of children's books that are on sale for the holiday season.

We are knelt on the floor surrounded by books when Jade looks up over my shoulder and sighs. "This man follows you everywhere, I swear."

"What do you mean?" I ask before turning my head to see Jack and Jordan walking towards us. "What are you both doing here? Don't you have a greasy full English breakfast waiting for you?"

Jack takes my hands in his and helps me stand.

"I wanted to check in on my girl. You haven't texted me back, and I was worried."

“Worried?” My brows pull together. I glance between him and Jordan quickly before continuing. “You walked me to the door this morning. You know how busy it gets on a Saturday. I don’t always have time to check my phone.”

“Yes, Olivia, but you could spare two minutes to check in and let me know how you are.” His gaze is so intense that I find myself captivated by his eyes.

“I’m fine. I promise. I am just super busy today.” I gesture to the mess around me.

“After what happened yesterday, I need to know we’re okay.”

I can't wrap my head around this man’s actions lately. Just yesterday, when I was desperate for some comfort, he refused to provide it, and now he’s standing in front of me, begging for the very same thing. To make matters worse, he kept me quiet all night long, and now he's broadcasting it to the world.

I open my mouth to speak but quickly close it again before I say something that could risk making him angry. I’m at work, so I must remain professional, and I get the feeling he knows that.

Jordan takes this time to look between both of us before asking, “Why? What happened yesterday?”

I turn to answer him, but Jack beats me to it again. “Olivia lost her temper. Didn’t you, Liv?”

My jaw drops in disbelief, and my eyes feel like they're about to pop out of my head. Before I can say anything, Jack turns to Jordan and says, “Come on, it doesn’t matter. Now that I’ve seen that she is ok we can go for breakfast.”

“Ok, you can buy the first round. Are you coming out with us after work?” Jordan turns to face me.

Out? No one told me anything about going out.

“I wasn’t aware anyone was out tonight.”

Jack lets out a small, humourless laugh. "I told you yesterday, Liv. We are going for breakfast and then we're staying out. Georgia and Daisy are meeting us a little later."

No. No, he did not. He told me he was meeting Jordan this morning for breakfast, but he never mentioned us going out. Or maybe he did? So much happened yesterday. Perhaps I just forgot.

"Ok, well yes, I can come out. I just need to go home and get sorted first."

"No." Jack snaps at me. "You take too long. Just go home and get changed and meet us. You don't need to spend hours on your hair and makeup. I prefer you as you are."

Before I can respond, he pulls me into him, kisses me, and turns to leave with Jordan hot on his tail. I think I have whiplash from his mood swings.

"Well?" Jade asks from behind me. "What happened yesterday? You were fine when I left you both."

I turn to look at her, still completely stunned. She already seems sheepish around Jack, so I decide to be honest with her but skip the parts that he wouldn't want me to disclose to anyone else.

"Nothing, I did nothing." I shake my head. "I asked him a question he didn't like, and it caused an argument."

"I'm sorry," she frowns, "you asked him a question, and lost your temper?" She looks down at the floor and mutters under her breath, "must have been one offensive question."

"Why don't you come with us? Tonight, I mean," I ask, looking for any way to change the topic of conversation from what happened last night. Jade and I never spend time outside of work, and I can see the confusion all over her face.

"I mean, I can if you would like me to. I can walk to yours when I'm ready, and we can go together because there is no chance I am walking into a pub full of strangers alone."

"Well, it's settled then. You can come in for a quick shot before we walk down."

"Fine. But I'm not stepping foot in that club. I'll come to the pub with you, and then when you guys move on, I'll go home."

"There is more to life than your bedroom walls, Jade."

"I'll have you know my walls are the most interesting thing in my life right now."

"And you don't see the issue with that?"

"Do you want me to come or not?" She hands me a stack of books she has stickered.

"Obviously I do, or I wouldn't have asked you."

"Then leave my boring life alone."

Relief washes over me. Not only have I managed to avoid talking about the events of yesterday, but I am also hoping that with Jade by my side, Jack will not mention anything.

We keep busy for the rest of the day. I fired a text to Jack on my lunch break to let him know Jade would be coming out with us. He thought it was a clever idea as she's the only eighteen-year-old we know that spends her weekends inside instead of going out with friends and letting her hair down. We spent a good hour discussing what we would wear and how we would do our hair and makeup. Even though Jack told me not to, there is not a chance I would be seen dead on a night out with a bare face and my hair on top of my head.

By the time we lock up, all of the children's books have been organised and stickered. We say goodbye to Maggie, thanking her for her help on the register today, then make our way home to get ready.

When I get home, I quickly shove some food down me to line my stomach. One thing I've learned as I've gotten older is that eating is definitely not cheating when it comes to nights out. Lining my stomach is a must! After my shower, I find myself staring at my reflection in the mirror, contemplating just for a moment whether to just get dressed and go as Jack suggested. The last thing I want is to spark another argument with him. It's then that I think back to the night we met.

Chapter 6

Before...

The sweltering, cramped atmosphere of this nightclub is almost unbearable. Georgia discreetly signals to me that she needs to go outside away from the stifling heat, so I follow her as she pushes through the dozens of sweaty bodies packed onto the crowded dance floor.

The club's layout features two distinct dance areas. One upstairs and one down. The downstairs floor caters to my personal music preferences, with its gritty emo vibe. Growing up I had every Green Day album, which my neighbours didn't appreciate in the slightest. That may be because I used to play them at maximum volume and scream along to songs. In contrast, the larger upstairs dance floor plays a selection of chart-topping and mainstream dance tracks.

Georgia and I typically start our nights upstairs, then move downstairs as the upper level becomes increasingly packed and difficult to navigate. However, tonight it seems we may need to head downstairs even earlier, as the upstairs area is already so crowded that it's almost impossible to breathe. Each dance floor has its own dedicated bar; the upstairs area does however have the added addition of flashing lights.

We make our way downstairs to get some fresh air as the club continues to fill up quickly. Jordan disappeared twenty minutes ago and never returned. Well, I'm guessing he didn't return, that or he couldn't find us through the crowd upstairs. He mentioned earlier when he popped into my work that his little brother Jack was coming out tonight. I immediately agreed to the night out because if you had seen the brother in question, you would have done the same. I should note that I only caught a brief glimpse of this brother, but that was more than enough for me to be convinced about the prospect of spending an evening with him.

Weaving our way through the sea of people, we manage to make it outside. Jordan is standing at a table in the corner with his brother, and he waves us over. Both brothers are wearing black skinny jeans and a black polo shirt. There is no doubt these two are related. Jordan is slightly taller than his brother Jack, but their features are almost identical.

We reach the table, and Jordan introduces us. The three of them soon fall into conversation whilst I stand there and just watch. This man is absolutely breathtaking. He stands tall, has dark features, and is incredibly attractive. His shirt clings perfectly to the muscles in his arms, as if it were tailored specifically to highlight their definition. His smile. That jaw dropping smile. His mouth showcases a set of straight, brilliantly white teeth. Dimples grace both of his cheeks. As I gaze up at his face, I meet his dark eyes, which are fixed intently on me. Quickly, I break the eye contact and look down at the table, but not before I can feel the blush travelling up from my neck to my face. The blush he most definitely noticed. I didn't get a chance to take him in properly earlier as I was too busy at work, but I swear this man was made by the gods. My body is screaming at me to look back at him, but my heart is telling me it's not ready to be broken again.

I try to focus on the conversation around me just in time to hear Georgia mention she is going back inside to get a drink. Jordan starts to follow her inside but turns to me. "Are you coming?"

"Not yet, I'll be in soon. I just need another minute." Another minute to pull myself together and stop acting like a child.

"I'll wait out here with her," I hear from across the table. I look up to find Jack still looking at me. His eye contact is so intense. I get instant butterflies just by looking at him.

Jordan gives us a thumbs up before going back inside with Georgia, leaving me alone with his brother.

"You don't have to wait with me. I'll be fine," I say, "I just need another minute."

He lets out a half laugh, so deep and raspy. “Tell me about yourself, Olivia. Tell me everything.” He places his elbows on the table and holds his head in his hands.

“I don’t think you have the time or the energy to hear about my life.” I look down at the suddenly interesting table between us.

“I don’t think you know enough about me to make that decision. Enlighten me, Olivia.”

I’m unsure if it’s the drink I have consumed, whether I have just had enough of hiding who I am, or the fact that I am so intimidated by him that makes me tell the stranger in front of me everything. I tell him about my birth father and all the pain he inflicted on my mother and me growing up. I tell him about being bullied throughout school and how hard it has been for me to gain my independence and confidence back. I tell him about my ex-boyfriends and how awful they have been and how many times my heart has been broken. To my surprise, he opens up just as much to me. He tells me about his job, his family, about his ex-girlfriend being unfaithful behind his back for half of their relationship and how much she broke him as a person.

When I check my phone, I realise we’ve been out here for an hour just talking to each other, like we’ve been friends for years and are just catching up. Talking to him feels so natural.

“We better go inside. They’ll be wondering where we are,” I tell him from across the table.

“After you.” He smiles and gestures for me to go in before him. *Such a gentleman.*

We find Jordan and Georgia upstairs and they both have drinks waiting for us. I must be back on the dance floor for all of ten minutes before Georgia pulls me off to the toilets.

“Where on earth have you been?” She inquires, applying another layer of lipstick in the club's less-than-pristine mirror.

“Downstairs… where you left me…” I quip, while attempting to tame my wild hair with a brush.

"I left you over an hour ago, Hun." She eyes me in the mirror. "Oh my god, you have the hots for the brother."

"I do *not* have the hots for him. I was talking to him about life. The conversation just flowed, but that was it."

"We could both marry a brother and finally be sisters! Oh, Liv, imagine the fun we would have!" She squeals at me.

"George, you know I'm not ready for that. I will not survive another heartbreak," I say to her as I turn to unlock the door and make my way back onto the dance floor.

We spent the rest of the night singing and dancing to the music. I tried my hardest to convince them we should go downstairs, but they insisted upstairs had a "better vibe." I made eye contact with Jack several times through the night, and I now know Georgia was right. I most certainly do have the hots for him, but who wouldn't? The man is beautiful. My heart is nowhere near ready to be broken again, though. I honestly don't know if I would be able to survive going through that pain. Trusting another person seems like an impossible task.

When the club closes, we stumble outside, and I say goodbye to my friends whilst they are still waiting for Jack to grab his jacket. I start my walk home, with my keys between my fingers in case anyone approaches me. Isn't it so disheartening that women feel compelled to take such precautions? Walking home alone shouldn't have to be such a risky thing. Does anyone even teach us, or is it just something we instinctively do?

I'm walking alone for what feels like the longest five minutes of my life when suddenly, I feel someone draping their jacket over my shoulders. I whip around, my fist clenched around my key, prepared to defend myself, only to find it's Jack.

"I'll walk you home. Jordan wouldn't forgive me if something happened to you."

I smile up at the man in front of me. Jordan always offers to walk me back, but he and Georgia live on the other side of town, so I always feel too bad. I don't like people making a fuss over me, but with the level of alcohol in my system and Jack in front of me, I'm not going to refuse. I turn around and start walking in the direction of my house.

"Thank you."

"No need to thank me, Olivia. To be totally honest, I just wasn't prepared to part ways with you yet."

"Well, I wasn't ready to part ways with you either," I tease as I nudge his shoulder.

"Are you really sure about that? You didn't stick around for me." He grins down at me.

"I don't wait for anyone. Especially when my bed is calling my name."

"I can't lie, I'm completely envious of that bed." He wraps his arm around my shoulders, drawing me closer.

He walks me to my front door, and when I go to take his jacket off my shoulders to give it back to him, he stops me. "Keep it. I have a feeling I will be seeing you again, Olivia."

THIS MAN!!! THIS CONFIDENCE!!!

He gently tucks a stray hair behind my ear, his fingers caressing my chin as he leans in to kiss me. Sparks fly through my body, and the butterflies in my stomach flutter so wildly they almost make me feel dizzy. The kiss is tender and sweet. He pulls his head back and smiles at me, showing me those dimples in all their glory. "Goodnight, Olivia."

"Goodnight, Jack."

He watches me go into the house and lock the door before leaving. Only when I am in my bed do I let myself believe that this could be something. I have never opened up to a man the way I have tonight with Jack. He makes me feel safe, and that's a feeling I constantly find myself chasing. Jack is right. I will definitely be seeing him again. I will crave seeing that smile every single day for the rest of my life. He is the final thing on my mind as I fall asleep, the smell of his aftershave still on my skin from wearing his jacket.

Chapter 7

I realise I am probably just overthinking. Surely, he's not going to be mad at me for wanting to look nice. I appreciate that he loves me and thinks I'm beautiful in my own skin, but I know he also thinks I'm pretty when I am all dolled up. If he didn't, then he would never have spoken to me that night.

I dedicate the next ninety minutes to getting myself ready. I have styled my hair in loose curls and applied my makeup just the way I like it, featuring winged eyeliner and eyeshadow that enhances the brightness of my eyes. Instead of the usual red lip, I choose to wear Very Victoria by Charlotte Tilbury tonight. This lipstick is undoubtedly my most treasured item. My mum gifted it to me for Christmas. She visited the store and inquired about the best recommendation for someone with my skin tone, and they truly nailed it. No other lipstick in existence complements my pale skin as beautifully as this one. I've never been inclined to use fake tan, and I will not start tonight, I wish more people felt comfortable in their real skin. I consider myself a low-maintenance girl, and the thought of having to scrub off a tan every week is simply not appealing to me.

This afternoon, as things began to calm down at work, I took a quick trip to the clothing store nearby and purchased a black playsuit. It has intricate lacing throughout, complemented by a black slip underneath. The cap sleeves effectively conceal the areas of my arms that I feel most insecure about.

One of the things I was bullied for as a child was my weight. The girls in my class decided to spread a rumour that I was anorexic. If anything, I was the opposite. I did everything I could growing up to try to gain weight, but no matter how much I switched my diet up, I stayed the same size. Nothing has changed now I'm an adult. I still struggle to maintain or gain any weight, which leaves me feeling insecure about the same things I was paranoid about all those years ago.

I grab my black clutch and go downstairs when I hear Jade knock.

"You look amazing," I say to her as she walks through the door into my dimly lit hallway. Her makeup is the same as it is at work, but she has added lipstick. It really is the only way to tell the difference between her daytime and nighttime look. She is wearing a long-sleeved, black body-con dress and a pair of strappy sandal heels.

"I believe you promised me a shot, and I am technically here ten minutes early, so I think I deserve two."

"At least you left your attitude at home this evening," I say to her with a raised eyebrow.

"Don't push me, White, or I will phone in sick for the next month and let you struggle," she says as she walks past me in the direction of my kitchen. I'm concerned for a moment about the fact she knows where my kitchen is until I remember she lives around the corner and all the houses on this estate have the same layout.

I can tell she's nervous, so if the girl wants two shots, then she will get them.

"You don't need to be nervous, you know," I pass her both of her shots, "they're not horrible people."

"I know that. It's just…" she cocks her head and sighs at me, "I heard things about Jack when he was single. How he treated a friend of mine. None of it was good, Liv."

"He is five years older than your friends. Are you sure it was him?" Surely, even he knows that a twenty-three-year-old sniffing around someone who is barely eighteen sounds slightly wrong.

"Positive. She showed me a picture when I told her you were with him. He got quite rough with her. Her dad walked in on them having an argument and saw him shove her. That's why they ended things. Her dad said he would break his legs if he ever touched her again."

My Jack. She must have done something to make him act that way, like I did when I asked him about Katie, or she could possibly be lying. Maybe he just lost interest in her because of her age, and she was upset. This would explain why she is so sheepish around him though.

"Thank you for the heads up, but he would never hurt me, Jade. Honestly, you don't need to worry."

We knock our shots back, taking one each for the journey to town and before I know it, we're walking into the pub. I immediately notice Jack sitting at a booth in the corner with Jordan, Georgia, Daisy, and Jordan's friend Dylan.

I have met Dylan before. He seems nice enough. In comparison to the others in the group, he is rather shy and reserved, yet he makes up for his shyness with his quick one-liners that have us all laughing uncontrollably. His hair is shoulder length and is so perfectly wavy it's almost annoying. He's another member of the ginger club, although his is a shade of strawberry blonde rather than auburn.

I walk Jade to the table, and Jack is the first one to glance up and see us. He gets up and approaches the pair of us. My anxiety hits me right away because I should have been here hours ago, but I wanted to ensure I looked good for him.

"I'm just going to get a round of shots. Join me?" He asks.

Quickly, I introduce Jade to the group and let her know that I'll be back as soon as I can. I feel terrible about leaving her with people she isn't familiar with, but when I glance back to see how she's doing, I notice she's already chatting with Dylan. He seems to be focused entirely on her. The drinks are clearly easing his shyness.

When I catch up to him, I find Jack at the bar paying for the round he promised our friends. He is still wearing the clothes he had on earlier, what I now call his trademark outfit, a pair of black skinny jeans paired with a white T-shirt, his usual chain around his neck and a watch on his wrist. He smells incredible- as always - with a hint of spice and sandalwood. Whenever I catch a whiff of him, it's like a wave of calm washes over me, and tonight is no exception. My nerves vanish as swiftly as they come.

“I wasn’t sure you were coming. But wow, Olivia, you look absolutely stunning tonight!"

There he is, the man who has my heart. The one who lifts me up and makes me feel fabulous. I glance down at myself and can't help but smile. "Thanks."

“Let’s have a good night tonight,” he looks concerned as he says, “I miss how we used to be.”

“I miss us too,” I admit to him.

“Please stop accusing me of things that I would never do to you.”

Now would not be the right time to bring up his fling with the eighteen-year-old, then?

“I will try better. I promise.”

“That’s all I need you to do.” He bends down to plant a gentle kiss on my forehead, his thumb softly brushing against my cheek.

We walk back from the bar towards the table full of our friends. This pub is our go to for breakfast, lunch, dinner, nights out, you name it, and we have been here for that reason. The drinks are cheap, and the food is good. It’s quite outdated decoration-wise. The patterned carpet is well-worn and stained with all kinds of substances. It’s the type of carpet that your parents would have had in the nineties, one they would match their curtains and sofa to, on purpose. The deep oak-coloured tables match the chairs perfectly.

When we are back with the group, I grab a chair from an unused table and settle at the end of the booth. Here, I can see all my friends and be involved in all conversations. Georgia and Daisy are deeply discussing whose week at work has been more stressful. I am going to say Daisy takes the crown for this one, considering she works for a law firm. Meanwhile, Jordan and Jack are chatting about tomorrow's football game and are making their predictions for who they think will win. Their dad supports the same team as them, and they make sure that they watch the game together every week, a little family tradition I would love to continue with Jack, if him and I ever had a son one day. Dylan and Jade are engaged in casual life conversations, getting to know one another, just like Jack and I did many months ago.

The thing about sitting back and observing people is you can see everything. People-watching is one of my favourite things to do, but tonight, something is off, and I can't quite place my finger on it. There is something about Jack and Dylan's behaviour that is odd. Not odd in a scary way, but they both seem more alert than normal, and chattier. I will find out what it is before the night is over. Once I set my mind to something, I always find the answer I'm looking for.

"Olivia, you would know," Daisy shouts at me across the table.

"I would know what?" I ask, turning my attention to my newest friend.

"How good are the Kylie lip kits? And are they worth the money?"

"I am telling you, no lipstick in the world is worth that kind of money." Georgia adds.

"I think so. I mean, I have other lip products that I use, but the Kylie ones seem to stay on my lips for longer, and they don't leave my lips feeling overly dry like some others do."

"I told you, George. The Queen of makeup herself has spoken." Daisy pokes at Georgia's chest.

"I forgot to ask you, Liv, actually, would you do my makeup for a date I have planned in a few weeks?" Georgia asks me.

I see Jordan's gaze shift towards her once she has finished speaking, and I can't help but feel a twinge of sympathy for him. However, if he isn't ready to express his true feelings to her, she is completely justified in moving on. Everyone deserves love in life, except for criminals, they do not deserve love. This excludes those who commit minor offenses but rather refers to the 'Ted Bundy' type criminals.

"Of course I will. Just let me know what you would like a few days before."

My love for makeup started as a teenager. I have always had a knack at applying my own makeup, yet I never really practised on anyone else until my mum asked me for help doing hers a few months ago. She had to go to her friend's wedding, and she asked me to do it for her, and if I do say so myself, it came out amazing.

I'm torn at the moment between training to be a makeup artist and finally doing something I know I love and something I'm truly passionate about, or staying at my job that I do love so very much but I don't see myself progressing any further in. I love making other people feel good, and I will never tire of people's reactions when they see themselves all dolled up.

We leave to set off to the club a few hours later. Jade has still decided she has had enough to drink at the pub, and I'm not going to be the person who forces her into a club she doesn't want to be in. So, Dylan is going to walk her home. I insisted she let me walk her, but she seemed to like the idea of the alone time with Dylan. For someone who was so concerned about a five-year age gap a matter of hours ago, she doesn't seem bothered about an eight-year age gap now. Georgia and Daisy each link an arm on either side of Jordan and walk a few steps ahead of me and Jack.

"I need to get some money out. You guys can walk ahead, I'll catch you up," I shout to the back of their heads.

I get the usual thumb up from Jordan and turn to put my card in the machine. Jack is beside me before I manage to get my card in.

"Oh, come on now, don't be ridiculous. I'm treating you tonight," he insists.

"Are you sure? I got paid, so I have the money."

"Of course, I am sure Liv. You don't need to pay for anything when I'm around. You know that."

"I do, but it just doesn't sit right with me when you pay for everything. It makes me feel a bit guilty."

"Baby, my job is way better, and I earn more than you do. If I want to spoil my girl, I will!"

I roll my eyes, knowing there's no point in arguing with him. Once he sets his mind on something, it's a done deal. The feminist in me is shouting, *'Don't let a man pay for you! You're a strong, independent woman!'* But the romantic in me is whispering, *'This feels like a scene from a fairytale.'*

As he extracts his wallet from the depths of his jeans pocket and flips it open to retrieve his card, a small bag tumbles to the ground. In that moment, the unsettling truth about his odd behavior hits me. I had promised myself I would uncover the reason behind their strange actions, yet this was the last thing I thought it could be. He crouches to retrieve the bag and tuck it back into his wallet, but before he can do so, I grab his arm and turn him towards me. When his gaze meets mine, I am struck by the sight of his pupils, unnaturally dilated, and the unsettling realisation that he is not really there, he's merely a shell of the man I love. His eyes feel like those of a stranger. How did I not see this before? A wave of nausea washes over me, and I begin to tremble almost immediately. Tears threaten to spill from the corners of my eyes. My breath comes in shallow, erratic gasps, and I struggle to articulate the words, "What have you done?"

"Nothing, it's not as bad as you think it is, Liv. You should try it sometime, then you will see." He snatches his arm back and continues typing his PIN number into the machine.

My brows pull together because he knows me. He knows this isn't something I want in my life. I get that people enjoy experimenting, and everyone has their own views on matters like this, but he knows me. He knows that this kind of thing frightens me.

"You know that won't happen, Jack. Like ever." My disappointment in him is overwhelming. I turn away, following the path my friends took. I need a moment alone to process everything. Are my friends all acting this way? A wave of dread washes over me as I realise, I left Jade with Dylan, who shares the same unsettling demeanor as Jack. I quickly pull out my phone, attempting to call her, but she doesn't pick up. I send her a text, hoping she's alright. *What will she think of me if she thinks this is the type of thing I allow the people I care about to do? What if she thinks I do this?*

I can hear him before I see him, he almost sounds like he's running to me, but I can't turn around, I can't stop walking. I feel like my heart is breaking into a thousand little pieces. How could he betray me like this? How could he betray us?

"Liv, just wait a minute." He grabs my arm tightly and spins me around to face him so fast I nearly lose my balance and fall, probably because of the drink I have consumed, but also because of the shock. He is grasping my arm so hard it hurts.

"Why would you do this, Jack?" Tears are streaming down my face now, and I think I might even be yelling.

"It's not what you think. I don't do it all the time, just occasionally when I'm under pressure. I told you I wanted to enjoy the night, Liv. Don't mess it up now. You promised you'd do better."

"You've done this before?" I demand. "When we were together? Have you done this while we have been together?"

"Yes," he replies, raking his hand through his deep brown hair, "yes, Liv, I have."

My knees start trembling. I have told him about my past, the men who have caused me pain, who have been involved with this kind of thing. He has held me more times than I can count, as I have told him about all the awful things I have witnessed because of addiction.

My friend passed away last year because of drugs. One foolish choice cost her everything. A girl I have known since I was four was taken from me right before my eyes. I still remember the moment it all went wrong. She had excused herself from the dance floor to go to the toilet. Twenty minutes later, when she hadn't returned, I took Lily's hand, and we made our way to the girls' toilets. We knocked on the door for another five minutes and got no response. Fortunately, there is a girl who works at the club who was more than helpful, and since that night, we have become very close friends. Natalia opened the register and gave us a coin to open the lock from the outside, and that's when my world turned upside down.

I pushed open the door, and there she was, lying on the floor, motionless, not breathing. At first, she looked like she was sleeping, that was until I got down close to her, and then I noticed how blue her lips were, and the vomit all down her chest and on the floor. I used my hand to brush her hair from her face, and her skin felt ice cold. I don't think I have ever screamed so loudly in my life. I was shaking her, slapping her face, yelling at her, but it was too late. She was gone.

When the paramedics arrived, they confirmed what I already knew. They also discovered the reason this happened still clasped tightly in her hand. Neither of us had any idea she had been taking something. If we had known, we would have taken it from her. If I had been ten minutes earlier maybe, just maybe, I could've saved her life. There is never a moment when I am in the club that I don't think about what happened there. Most nights, Jack and I leave early because it becomes too overwhelming for me. He then holds me all night while I cry into his chest, consumed by the what ifs.

That very reason is why I never would have thought in a million years that Jack would be so reckless. I know that it's not worth arguing with him, not if he has taken something. You can never predict how a person might behave when influenced by substances like drugs, yet I also cannot abandon him. What if I go home and leave him alone, and the same thing happens again while I'm not around?

I just shake my head at him and turn to walk towards the club that my friends are in. He follows behind me, but we don't speak. The walk is long enough that I can compose myself, put on my best fake smile, and face the world. I call it my customer service face. The face I put on when someone comes into the store with an attitude. We pay to hang our coats up, and I weave through the crowd upstairs to find my friends. One quick look at them, and I know they haven't touched anything, *thank God.*

I spend the rest of my night dancing with my girls, singing to songs and avoiding Jack where possible. When we leave, I check my phone and see Jade has texted me back and she is fine. She said Dylan was the perfect gentleman. He walked her to her door, they exchanged numbers, and then he left. At least that's one of my problems sorted. Now, I just have to make it through this walk home with Jack.

We walk hand in hand in silence for a while before he stops. I turn to face him, and I can see his eyes are full of regret. I let out a big breath and walk to him. Holding his face in my hands, I reach up and kiss him. He kisses me back, and it's passionate and full of unspoken apology. His own hands come up to cup my face as he breaks the kiss between us. He rests his forehead on mine. We stand like this for a while, just holding each other close. I love him. I love him unconditionally, just as he loves me and all my flaws. We will work through this together and come out on top like we always do because we are infinite. There is not another person on this earth that I am meant to spend my life with. Jack is it for me.

"I am begging you, Jack, please do not do this again."

"Just because it happened to her doesn't mean it will happen to me, Liv."

"How often are you doing it?" I ask.

"Too often lately. I do it to distract myself from my life. I will try, ok? I will try to stop because I love you."

"I love you too."

Chapter 8

Before…

Jack and I have been together for a month today. He sent me a message this morning to tell me he would come over and look after me. I'm not exactly unwell, but I'm just having an off day. I have these days more often than not now. It isn't a surprise to me that I have my struggles with mental health some days. After everything I've endured, it almost feels like a given.

My mum and dad have been incredible, doing their best to help me through it all. I depend on medication every day now to keep things under control, yet even that doesn't always seem to help. I really should book a doctor's appointment and speak to someone. I know I should, but when things start to get bad again, the people I love always find a way to pull me out of the pit I have fallen in. It's also more challenging than some people think it is, talking to a stranger about your life. Telling them about the dark thoughts that plague your mind.

Before I started medication, there were days I couldn't even get out of bed. I wouldn't eat, I wouldn't shower. I would just sleep. It isn't like I have sat back and done nothing about it. I've tried the endless workshops that the local mental health service has recommended I do, but honestly, they do nothing. They just tell me how I can manage my anxiety and depression, they don't actually let me talk to someone, which I believe is what I need.

Today, though, I have managed to get up and have a shower, which means I've accomplished something. I've tied my long, messy hair up into a ponytail on top of my head, giving me a free face lift. I've washed my face and applied minimal skincare. The only clothes that I will wear in this kind of mood are my high-waisted black leggings and my mum's old, oversized football jumper with a pair of fluffy socks, the kind you get for Christmas every year. I haven't eaten yet, but when Jack arrives, I'm sure he'll try to coax me into eating something.

Thirty minutes go by, and then there's a knock at my front door. I drag myself from my spot on the sofa and pause the TV. I'm halfway through the new season of Teen Mum UK. They inspire me, they were only children themselves when they had their children, yet here they are, a few years on, with successful lives. When society tells them they will never get anywhere in life, they are out here working their arses off to prove them wrong. When I unlock and open the door, Jack is standing there with a bunch of red roses and a bag full of stuff.

"I got you these," he hands me the flowers, "and I also picked up a load of sugar for you to eat." He opens the bag, then for me to look inside, and it is full of all my favourite snacks.

I must be the luckiest girl in the world to have a man as good as this in my life. Most of my ex-boyfriends have stayed away when I'm like this, scared of my mood swings, but Jack takes time out of his day to pick up my favourite things, then insists he comes and sits with me. This man knows me better than I know myself.

"Thank you." I manage to get out. My throat is so dry, my voice is barely there.

"Anything for my girl." He pulls me into him and holds me by the front door, kissing the top of my head.

I pull away from him and look into those deep brown eyes, that always make me feel better instantly.

After putting the roses into a vase, I take the bag to the living room and find Jack sitting waiting for me on the sofa, TV controller in one hand and a blanket in the other. I sit in the spot next to him and cuddle up to him. He covers me with the blanket and kisses the top of my head. He already knows when I get like this, that I do not like to talk to anyone, so we sit in silence, watching the TV.

After a few hours have passed by I feel myself getting sleepy. Jack is stroking my hair. We have eaten almost all of the snacks he bought over with him and honestly, I am feeling better. As my eyes start to get too heavy to stay open, I hear him whisper, “I love you, Olivia White. More than you will ever know.”

It's the first time he has told me he loves me, and it’s when I’m at my very worst. It hasn’t scared him off. It has made him care about me even more.

Chapter 9

When we finally walked home, we had a conversation about the events of tonight and how we were each feeling. I expressed to Jack that I didn't like him being involved with things like drugs after seeing what they can do to a person. I told him I couldn't stand to live in a world where he didn't exist anymore. I told him I need him more than I let on. My entire life, I have tried to be independent and carry the weight of my past on my shoulders, scared to burden those around me with my demons, but when I met Jack, he made me feel so safe I told him about it all, and since then I've depended on him a fair bit. He took my demons and made them his own.

Jack told me how he was feeling. He has been worried that I will leave him because we keep having disagreements. He likes to be in control of everything in his life, and when he loses that control, it causes him to spiral and do things he is not proud of. He admitted to me he thinks he may be addicted to the drugs he has been taking on the sly and has promised me he will try to stop. I tried to reassure him, tell him that I'm not going anywhere because I love him with everything that I am.

I told him I would try better to be more open and understanding about the things that I say, so I don't make him feel this way again. I would do anything to make him happy. It's my job as his girlfriend to make him feel that way.

We got back to my house, and I changed into one of Jack's t-shirts, and we got into bed. We fell asleep holding each other. Love like this only comes once in a lifetime. It is the type of love you read about in books. It truly is infinite. We would do anything for each other.

———

I'm not entirely sure what the time is when my eyes flutter open, the room is still pitch black which tells me I haven't been asleep for very long. I attempt to move so I can get more sleep, but I'm stuck. Lying on my stomach with my hands pinned beneath my body. As I lift my head from the pillow, a strong hand pushes it back down, it is then I realise the heaviness, the reason I cannot move is Jack on top of me. A wave of dread washes over me, settling deep in my stomach.

"Jack," I mumble into the pillow, "Jack please."

"I love it when you say my name," he whispers softly into my ear.

His lips begin to trail kisses down my neck, one of his hands fisted in my hair to keep my head pinned down whilst the other roams over my body.

"I don't want to. Please stop."

"Shh baby. You don't have to do any of the work you just lay there like a good girl for me," his breath is warm against my neck.

He shifts the hand that was pinning my head down to flip me beneath him, so I am facing him. Stradling me, he reaches to his right where he retrieves the belt he wore tonight. I try to struggle, to get away from him, but he is far stronger than I am. He grabs both of my hands and binds them with the black leather belt.

"Jack please, this isn't you. Please. You don't have to do this," I plead desperately.

"Shut up. You're ruining this for me," His left hand strokes my cheek, "your body is mine, Olivia."

Before I can protest, he reaches to his left and rummages through my bedside table, and then he shoves a pair of balled-up socks into my mouth, leaving me unable to speak. Panic starts surging within me. Any cries for help I can get out fall on deaf ears as Jack strips me of my underwear. Tears leak from my eyes as the horrifying realisation sinks in, he will not stop. Most men are like this, they take everything from you. As long as they get what they desire, they remain indifferent to the pain they inflict.

He holds my tied hands tightly against my body as he forces himself into me. "That's it baby. You know you want this too."

I have never experienced pain like it. Every thrust brings further pain. My body goes limp below his. I have no fight left in me.

The sun is up, and I haven't slept at all. I'm sitting here in my bed, with my knees pulled to my chest, watching the man I have given my all to sleep peacefully beside me like nothing has happened. I feel numb. My alarm is due to go off in five minutes, and then I will have to face him before I go to work, but I don't want to face him. *Is this the effect the drugs have on him?* I make the decision to turn my alarm off but when I grab my phone, I see a message from Natalia, my friend that works at the club.

Nat: Are you ok? I saw you stood in the street last night when I was on my way home from work.

The truth is I was ok when she saw me last night. Am I ok now, though? No, no, I am not.

Me: I'm ok, we had a bit of a disagreement, but it was sorted by the time you saw us.

I get out of bed and as quietly as possible pick out my uniform for the day and grab my towel for a shower before work. I have a feeling one shower will not be enough to wash last night off me. My body feels dirty. I don't even want to look at it, let alone touch it while washing myself.

I tiptoe down the hallway into the bathroom and lock the door. Then I exhale deeply, and the tears I had somehow kept at bay for the past hour escape from my eyes. It feels like it was just a nightmare. *Could he actually do that to me?* The blood and bruises tell me that yes, he could.

Somehow, I manage to get through my entire morning routine without waking Jack up. My parents will not mind him still being here whilst I'm at work. In fact, my dad has questioned it many times. He doesn't understand why he leaves when I leave. He basically lives here anyway, he only goes home to have a shower, so he doesn't run my mum's water bill up. All of his clothes are here as well as toiletries for the odd occasion he will wash here.

Since I've somehow slipped out of the house without disturbing anyone, I've decided to indulge in a large coffee instead of my regular medium. As I enter the coffee shop, I spot Rose at the counter chatting with Rob. I freeze in place, contemplating whether to turn around and leave, but she catches sight of me from the corner of her eye and turns to face me.

"There you are. Rob said you have usually been in by now. I was starting to worry I had messed the day up and you would be off today," my sister says, walking towards me.

Rose and I are opposite in every way. She is petite, with short chocolate brown hair. Her eyes are the same colour as our mum's, she has a tiny button nose that I have always been jealous of. She is wearing a dusty pink maternity jumper dress, that clings to her growing baby bump and of course her signature Crocs. Although the outfit wouldn't be my first choice, I hope I look this good when I'm pregnant. She is glowing.

She is in front of me now frowning, "Earth to Olivia. Hello?"

"Sorry," I say, shaking my head, "rough night, so I'm running a little late today. How are you? How is our girl cooking?" I say the only thing I can think of that I know will prevent us getting into conversation about me or my life. My sister's baby will be the first baby of the next generation in our family. Everyone is unbelievably excited.

Rose rubs a hand over her belly. "She is fine. I was finding you to tell you they have agreed to induce me early because I'm in so much pain. Obviously not yet but they said they will do it at 37 weeks," she is squealing by the time she has finished talking.

"That's amazing news. Have you told Mum yet?" Knowing our mum, she will be overjoyed to know her granddaughter will be here sooner than we expected her to be.

“No, I am on my way over there now, actually. She just texted me to say she is up, and I should go for breakfast, so I must run, but do not be a stranger, ok? I never see you anymore.”

She rolls up onto her toes and pats me on the head before she walks past me to leave.

“I love you,” I shout after her, and she blows me a kiss in return.

Coffee in hand, I walk into the staff room and put on my customer service face. My manager is over today. She only comes twice a week to make sure everything is running smoothly. She manages two different branches, and the other one apparently requires more attention than this one, but in all honesty, I think she avoids coming here because it’s a longer commute. When she does come over, she acts as my second mother. We know a lot about each other's lives. For instance, I know she will only buy the same brand of car when she needs a new one, if it isn’t a Kia she isn’t interested. She has a boyfriend she has been with for over twenty years. They have no children together because they don’t want any. She has a sister she sees a few times a year, she’s never gone into much detail about her sister, but I do know they had a falling out a while back and since then they seem to avoid each other where they can. The only time they really get together now is when they spend time with their mum.

We spend a good hour catching up with each other when she comes over, and then we spend the rest of the day working hard. Do not get me wrong, I work hard when she isn’t here, but when she is here, it’s a different level of demanding work, and the distraction is welcome today.

Before we get to work, I fire Jack a quick message to tell him that Cindy is over today and, therefore, I won’t have a chance to speak to him. Hopefully, this is enough to keep him away while I sort my head out. He’s scared of Cindy and her mood swings. I put my phone back in my bag, take a deep breath and walk out onto the shop floor, where Cindy has opened already.

Cindy is much older than me. She is in her late sixties but still works full-time, even with her arthritis. Some days, she can only use her right hand as her left is too sore, but she never lets it hold her back and stop her from doing what she must do that day. She is tall and slim with short, spiky grey hair. She has had hair like this for a long time now. I know because I've often stalked her social media to try and find a picture of her from when she was younger. I have come to the conclusion she has had the same hair style for her entire life.

As a manager, she doesn't have to wear the usual uniform the rest of us do. Instead, she wears a black fitted formal dress, with a pair of black tights and her signature Sketchers. She has a pair of those glasses that change depending on whether she is inside or outside, glasses and sunglasses in one pair.

I am lucky to have the manager that I do, I don't know many people that have a good relationship with their manager. The other girls that work here do pick on me for it, calling me Cindy's favourite, and if they ever need to ask her something they make me do it for them because she apparently never says no to me. I'm sure she has said no in the past, but I'm a pathological people pleaser, so I tend to do whatever it takes to make others happy. Therefore, it is likely I have never asked her anything that she could say no to.

I take over from her at the till whilst we wait for one of the other staff members to get here and take over. The problem with these big corporate companies is they expect you to get a list of a million things done in one day but refuse to spare you any added hours so you can get extra staff in to help.

By the time lunchtime comes around my feet are throbbing. My back is aching. I have what feels like thousands of tiny paper cuts on my hands. That's probably the biggest problem with this job. Working with paper in many different forms guarantees you at least one paper cut a day.

I take my bag and go out the back door of the store to sit in the fresh air. Here, there is less chance that someone will come and ask me something or interrupt my lunch. I change where I go on my lunch break often, so they will never find me in the same spot twice. It isn't very picturesque out here. I sit on a pallet from one of our old deliveries next to the bin. This is still better than having to talk to people though, especially today. I pull my phone out and check the messages that have come through.

Nat: Ok, you know where I am if you need me.

I smile at my phone. I haven't known her for as long as I have some of my other friends, but since everything that happened last year, she has been an angel. She is always there for me, no matter what.

Me: Thank you, angel girl. When are you off work next? Maybe we can have a girl's night?

Right now, a girl's night sounds so incredibly appealing. Speaking of girl's nights, I also have a message from Lily checking in because I have gone MIA.

Lily: Are you alive? Do I need to call the police?

Me: I am alive. Just busy with work and life

Lily: Life being that boyfriend of yours? He is too selfish I never see you anymore.

Me: How about you come over one night with Nat, and we have a night of films, gossip, and snacks?

I continue scrolling through my notifications, which are mostly full of spam emails and Facebook and Snapchat, telling me I have a memory to look back on, that I can fully say with my hand on my heart that I do not want to look at, but I love the enthusiasm. Then, at the very bottom is a message from Jack.

My heart feels like it's in my throat, I managed to go the entire morning without thinking about what happened last night, so engrossed with my work. I wish I had just continued working and not bothered taking a break, but Cindy would never allow such a thing.

Jack: Hey, beautiful. Thank you for letting me sleep in. I needed it. When you get home, pack a bag for a few days. I have told your mum and dad we will be going away for some alone time.

Me: Away where exactly? What about my job?

My phone buzzes almost at once.

Jack: I just got off the phone with Cindy. She said you're taking your lunch break outside. Why? Anyway, she said it was fine, and you deserve the time away.

As much as I want to argue and say I would rather stay at home and solve this, I do think he's right. Some time away from here will allow us to talk through everything properly with no outside influences. We are anything but ok at the moment, but I will do anything to get us there, including having these difficult conversations.

Me: Ok, I will pack when I'm home. When do we leave?

Jack: I will meet you from work. I'm just packing my stuff up now, and once you are home and packed, we will leave.

I lock my phone again and put it back into my bag, only a few more hours of work to get through and then we can start moving forward together. I will be telling him that last night was completely unacceptable and I'm not entirely sure how I move forward from that. I think he has planned this time away to try to apologise for his actions. Well, I *hope* he plans on apologising anyway.

Chapter 10

The rest of the day goes by much faster than I would like it to. As much as I'm excited to see Jack, I'm also scared. Cindy has finished locking up and said her goodbyes to me. She told me she doesn't want to see me again this week, that I can have the entire week off paid. Jack said he would meet me from work, but I can't see him anywhere, so I pull my phone out to call him.

"Hey, sorry, babe, I'm running late."

"That's fine. Should I just walk home and meet you there?"

"Yeah, go home and get packed, and I will meet you when I'm ready."

"Ok, I will see you in a bit."

I pull my phone away from my ear to end the call, but I hear him say, "I love you, Liv."

I freeze, unsure how to go about this. I do love him so very much, but I don't want him to think everything is ok when it isn't. So, I hang up and make my way home.

When I arrive home, my mum is busy in the kitchen getting dinner ready for her and my dad, who will be back from work soon. She has freshly washed hair, I can tell, because it's still damp, and it has turned into a frizzy, curly mess. I do prefer my hair curly, but I would much rather do it with a curling wand than spend the time adding the hundreds of products it would need to tame it naturally. She obviously has more patience than I do.

"Hey, baby. Jack not with you?" Mum asks whilst seasoning her traybake of various vegetables, this tells me she is making some form of soup that my dad will moan about. If the food is not a shade of beige, then I can guarantee he won't enjoy it.

I put my work bag on the back of the chair and walk over to give her a hug. I didn't realise how much I needed this hug. Yet again I am in a position where I want to tell my mum everything that happened, but I know if I do then that will be the end of me and Jack. I'm not ready for this to be the end of us.

"No, not yet. He's running late. I need to go and pack, and he said he will be here when I'm finished."

"It's nice of him taking you away for a few days. Very romantic," she says as she wiggles out of my hold to turn her attention back to her vegetables, oblivious to the pain that is eating me alive inside. "Did Rose tell you the news?"

"Yes, I saw her this morning when I went in to grab a coffee. It is extremely exciting, isn't it?"

"I need your dad to decorate the spare room, so we have room for her to stay over."

"You do know she isn't going to stay here for a long while yet, don't you?" I ask, raising my eyebrow at her.

"You are as bad as your father, you know that? Why can't you both let me enjoy this."

I chuckle at her. My mum is probably more excited about the new baby than my sister and Rob are. She cried when Rose told her she was having a baby and then again when she knew it was going to be a little girl. Rose and I come from a generation of just women. My nan has voiced many times how she would like us to have boys as she only has granddaughters. *No pressure or anything*. I have always pictured myself being a mum to boys. I think it would be so much fun, dinosaurs, and superheroes. It would certainly be different to the Barbies we grew up with.

"Of course, you can be excited. I'm just making sure you know she will not be living here."

"Well, I know that. Don't you have packing to do?"

I steal a carrot from her tray and make my way upstairs to my room. I don't actually own a suitcase, which yes, I know is abnormal. I only have a bright pink holdall bag. It really is a Mary Poppins bag though. It isn't overly large, but it holds everything I need, no matter where I go. I must have had it for nearly ten years now, and it's still going strong. Because I have no idea where we're going, I have no idea what to pack. I assume it will be in this country, well I sure hope it is anyway, so I pack the things I would usually wear in this weather. One pair of black high-waisted jeans, two pairs of ribbed leggings, one pair black and the other a chocolate brown colour. My favourite Taylor Swift jumper from her Era's Tour merch which is a charcoal grey with the Era's Tour poster printed on the back in black. I throw in a few oversized T-shirts, my Adidas trainers and Adidas socks. To finish it off I have added underwear, PJs, and a wash bag full of skincare, hair care and makeup.

Once I have finished packing, I sit on my bed and check my phone to see if Natalia or Lily have responded.

You have been added to the group chat Girls on Tour

Lily: Hello, ladies. I thought it would be easier to plan a night together if we were in one chat.

Nat: Read my mind. What about next weekend?

Lily: I can do Saturday?

Nat: I am meant to be working, but my boss owes me a night off, so it will be fine.

Nat: Are we staying in, or are we going to end up going out? I need to know if I need to buy something to wear

Lily: I think we should go out. Just girls though!

Nat: Liv?

I smile at my phone. I am so lucky to have these chaotic girls in my life. I should have known they would prefer to go out rather than stay in and watch a film. Lily doesn't have a boyfriend at the moment, so she is living her twenties the way they should be lived, making mistakes and having fun. Navigating this new thing called adulthood.

Me: Saturday is fine. I'm going away for a few days with Jack, but I will be back by then. Let's get dressed up and make it a night to remember.

Lily: You never said you were going away?

Me: In my defence, I didn't know about it until a few hours ago.

Nat: Oh my god, how romantic!!! Be safe. Use a condom.

This girl. The thing Nat and I bonded over most was our humour. The girl has had me bent over, unable to breathe from laughter, tears streaming from my eyes. We both had difficult upbringings, and I always find those who have been through the wringer tend to have a better sense of humour than those who have had the perfect life. Natalia was in care when she was younger before she was adopted by her now parents. I don't push her too hard and ask for all the gory details, but from the personal things she has told me, she has really been through it.

I am so engrossed in my phone I don't hear Jack knock and come in, until my mum is shouting at me from downstairs. I quickly check myself in my mirror before grabbing my bag and walking downstairs, where Jack is stood waiting for me, and my mum is beaming from beside him.

He is wearing a pair of jogging bottom fabric shorts and a plain white T-shirt. His hair has not been styled, so it has flopped onto his forehead. I decide at that moment that a relaxed Jack might be my favourite look yet. Annoyingly, it makes it harder to stay angry at him. It does however make me glad that I chose to wear a pair of black cycling shorts and a cropped Nike jumper. The shorts are high-waisted enough that they cover the bruises forming on my stomach and the sleeves from the jumper cover those on my wrists from the belt. My hair is still up in a high ponytail from work.

"Jordan let me borrow his car because mine still isn't fixed," he says as I eye the car key in his hand with confusion.

"Ok." I step from the last step and give my mum and big hug and kiss before opening the door for us to leave.

"Have fun, you two," my mum shouts from behind me.

I walk in front of Jack in silence as he grabs my bag from my hand. "Are you going to tell me what is wrong, or am I going to have to guess?"

I slide into the passenger side of the car and wait for him to put my bag in the boot along with his and climb in beside me before talking.

"What do you think is wrong, Jack?"

"If I knew Liv, then I wouldn't be asking, would I?"

I let out a small, humourless laugh and look him in the eye. "If someone tells you they do not want to have sex with you, Jack, it means no."

The shock on this man's face is unbelievable. His eyes have doubled in size, and his eyebrows have practically disappeared into his hairline.

"I have no idea what you are on about."

"Last night!" I am shouting now.

"We didn't have sex last night, Liv."

"Yes. We. Did." I say behind my clenched teeth. "I woke up with you on top of me, I told you to stop, and you chose not to. If it didn't happen Jack, then where have these bruises come from?" I roll the sleeves of my jumper up and roll the top of my shorts down to show him.

"I was asleep, Liv. If I do something in my sleep, I have no control over it." He reaches across the car to take my hand in his as his other comes up to cup my cheek. "I am sorry if that happened. You know I wouldn't do that to you on purpose."

Letting out a long, hard breath, I lean into his touch and close my eyes. "You scared me, Jack. I will not put up with it again."

He starts the car, types an address into the maps app on his phone and starts driving. "That isn't me, Liv. You know it isn't. Don't make up a version of me in your head. I am not a villain."

Deep down, I know he isn't. His heart is too big, and he cares too much to do something so awful to the person he loves on purpose. I decide to think it was all a dream instead of my reality. Most of my dreams are nightmares anyway. To avoid speaking about the matter any further, I close my eyes and rest my head against the window, hoping that when I wake up, we are somewhere that isn't here.

Chapter 11

Before...

I have just finished going to the toilet. I pull my black tights up, and my navy-blue denim dress down and wash my hands. This is my favourite outfit at the moment. My mum got it for me a few weeks ago. She said I had been so well-behaved when I was going to school that she thought I deserved a treat. I think she is right. I have been good at going to school. Even though the girls there are mean to me, I try to ignore them and get on with the day. I enjoy school. My teacher has had to give me English and Maths work from the year above because I am so clever. Richard is here today. I don't know how he found us or if my mum invited him over, but he is here.

Everywhere I turn, he is there. I do not want him here. The courts don't seem to care about that, though. They say I'm too young to have an opinion, that I'm not old enough to know what I do and do not want for myself. They are wrong. I know there is still a lot I don't know at the age of seven, but I do know that I do not want this man in my life anymore. He scares me. He thinks he can walk in and out of my life and expect me to forgive him and forget about all the hurt he has caused, but he can't. Children's first memories should be happy ones; ones they can look back on and tell their children about when they are older. Mine is anything but that. He took my happiness away from me when he made me and Rose sit and watch him hurt our mum.

I finish drying my hands on our ocean-blue hand towel and turn to look at myself in the mirror. I don't see much of my dad when I look at myself, I only see the various parts of my mum, and that makes me happy because she is the prettiest lady I have ever seen. My hair is tied up into pigtails. They look quite silly now that I'm looking at them. I asked for my hair to be cut short into a bob just like my mum's, but because it is so short, it looks silly now it's up. My pigtails don't hang the way they should. Instead, they poke up in all different directions. My mum told me this morning I should plait it, but I insisted on having it in pigtails. She always does know best. Next time, I will listen to her.

I hear the bathroom door open, and as I look behind my shoulder in the mirror, I can see him standing there. He comes in and shuts the door behind him. His smile even creeps me out. "There you are," he says.

I wake up drenched in sweat, yet I find myself unable to move. My body is frozen. I struggle desperately to move my arms, my legs, my head, but nothing will move. My eyes are wide open, but my body is still asleep. I attempt to call out Jack's name, but no sound manages to escape me. I catch something moving out of the corner of my eye. It looks like a person stood there, but I can't move to confirm. Tears start to leak from my eyes as the figure comes closer to my bed. I am screaming inside, but no one hears me. I shut my eyes tightly and try to wake up from this nightmare. I must be dreaming. This is not happening to me.

I keep trying to move my limbs when I open my eyes once more, but nothing changes. I am trapped here. To make matters worse, the shadowy figure that was lurking in the darkness is Richard. He is stood over me now, grinning. He is so close that I can almost taste the alcohol on his breath. He looks just as I remember from when he added me on Facebook years ago. Bald, with decayed teeth, and wrinkles etched into every part of his face. His years of drinking have taken a toll on him. He wears a pair of blue denim jeans, clearly old and worn, along with a grey long-sleeved T-shirt, the top button undone. I try to scream again, but still, no sound comes out. I am stuck here frozen whilst he puts his hands on my face. He says nothing as he bends down, smiling at me. He uses his left hand to tuck my hair behind my ear, and then I am sucked into the blackness again.

I wake up and sit upright in my bed. My breathing is shallow and quick. I take a moment to look around my room. The figure that was here earlier has vanished. The only people in my room now are me and Jack. *Jack.* I shake him awake as my tears stream down my face. He stirs and reaches his hand out to my pillow. When he finds it empty, he props himself up on his elbow.

"Liv," he says my name like it is a question.

"He was here," I say between my sobs, my entire body jolting with each one. "He was here. He touched me."

"Who?" he asks me, sitting upright now.

"Richard. He was here. In my room, I tried screaming, but..." I can't finish my sentence. I let the crying take over and Jack pulls me onto his lap. He brushes my hair with his fingers whilst whispering reassurances into my ear.

Once I have calmed down enough to speak, I tell him about my flashback dream and what happened when I woke up, well half woke up, I guess. To make me feel better, he does a quick sweep of the house and checks the doors and windows to make sure they are locked. I ask him to check every hiding place I can think of, and he checks them all without judging me once. He isn't here after all. It was all in my head. I have never had sleep paralysis before, in fact, I had never even heard of it before tonight, but Jack tells me it is perfectly normal for those who have experienced trauma. I certainly never want it again. I have never felt so useless and afraid.

When he gets back into bed, he pulls my body into his and holds me tightly against his chest. I breathe his smell in to calm myself. In his arms, I feel safe. He would never let him hurt me again. After a while, I manage to compose myself enough to stop crying completely, but I don't let go of him. I stay like this in his arms, falling in and out of sleep until the sun comes up.

Chapter 12

Jack wakes me when we get to our destination. It's dark outside, and I still have no idea where we are or how long we have been in the car for. When I check my phone, we have been driving for two hours.

"Where are we?" I ask as I rub my eyes.

"A little lodge I found online. It has a hot tub," he says, giving me a playful eyebrow raise.

"I didn't bring anything I need for a hot tub."

"You don't need anything. It's private no one can see us," Jack chuckles as he unbuckles his seatbelt to get out of the car and get our bags. I do the same and follow him to the boot, taking in my surroundings as I do.

"Did you bring me out here to kill me?"

"Excuse me? I treat you to a nice trip away and you take that as me trying to kill you?"

"I don't know what you're capable of anymore," I mutter to myself as I walk away from him.

From what I can see in the late evening light, we're at a lake. The moonlight dances on the surface of the water. It is so beautiful. The sky is clear, and the absence of light pollution allows the stars to twinkle brilliantly above. Dotted along the lake are several other lodges. I turn around to face our home for the next few nights and gasp. A rich oak lodge with a cosy deck that wraps around it stands before me. I walk up the three steps until I'm looking through the window. The space inside is compact and lit up by fairy lights. From what I can see, there's a double bed covered in black bedding with coordinating black and silver cushions, a few cupboards, along with a sink, and a microwave on the petite countertop. A large flatscreen TV is mounted to the wall, pointing to the bed, and at the very back of the space is a door, which I am guessing takes you to a bathroom. Well, I am hoping. I step back and walk around the side of the deck to the back that overlooks the lake, where I see a small hot tub and a wicker table with two chairs.

I have said to Jack before how I would love to come somewhere like this. I used to love camping as a child, but have since learnt to rely on warmth and comfort too much to go anymore. The lodges you can stay in now are more secluded than you would be when you go camping, with those added luxuries, you'd rather not live without. The main ones being your own toilet and shower.

"Beautiful, isn't it?" Jack says from behind me.

I walk to him and wrap my arms around his neck, looking into those eyes that consume me. "It is. I love it. Thank you."

"You don't have to thank me, Olivia. We need this time away." He leans down to kiss me passionately. When he pulls back, I see that smile. The one that reaches his eyes and highlights his dimples, one that I haven't seen in what feels like forever. He looks so young when he smiles like this, so carefree. He wiggles out of my hold and reaches for my hand to lead me to the front door. When he unlocks the door, he stands to the side to let me in first. *Such a gentleman.*

After further exploration, I can tell you now that the door at the very back does indeed lead to a bathroom. It has a large white tub that is big enough for two people, a toilet, and a sink. The floor is black and sparkly, like the bed.

I finished unpacking our bags whilst Jack went into the nearest town to get us a takeaway for dinner. He called me whilst he was out to tell me the very few options available, but we decided on Chinese in the end. We're now sat on the bed stuffing our faces, as it's too cold to sit on the decking, and there's no other seating inside. We have a regular Chinese order that we stick to no matter where we are. Jack has a chicken curry with egg fried rice and a chicken Chow Mein. I share his Chow Mein and egg fried rice, but I also order Hong Kong style sweet and sour chicken with a portion of chips. Jack never orders chips for himself, but he always, without fail, helps himself to half of mine when we start eating.

"I've arranged to meet Lil and Nat when we're back, by the way. They wanted a girl's night."

"Anyone would think they don't like me."

A small chuckle leaves me. "You know that isn't true. They just don't get to spend as much time with me as they used to. I am in high demand these days."

Jack takes my empty plate for me and leaves them in the sink to wash up later. He comes back and joins me on the bed, sitting opposite me, cross-legged so our knees touch. He takes my hands in his. "We need to talk, Liv."

I let out a big sigh and look into those soul-searching eyes. "I know we do. I don't want us to lose what we have, Jack. I can't live without you. I need you in my life."

"I know, Liv. I need you in my life as well. Sometimes, though, I feel like you don't take my feelings into consideration. I feel like you only care about yourself. I can't be with someone who doesn't try to see things from both sides."

"I do try, Jack. If you don't feel that way, then I'm sorry. I'll try harder. I never want you to feel like I don't appreciate you because I do."

"Your friends put ideas in your head, Liv. It's almost like they don't want us to be together."

"No one has put anything in my head, Jack." I squeeze his hands tighter. "The girls just don't want to see me get hurt, and before you and I were together, I used to spend a lot more time with them than I do now."

"Would you rather spend time with them than me?" He asks me. Looking between each of my eyes, searching for the answer.

"No," I say instantly. "I love spending time with you. You know that I do."

"Then I need you to start taking accountability, Liv. Stop making out that I am doing all these horrible things to you. It's in your head," he reaches a hand up to my cheek, "please, Liv. For us."

"Of course," I lean into his touch, "I'm sorry I made you feel this way. I will try better."

"I'm ok with you going out with them this time, but in the future, I think we need to spend our time together, no more going out and getting drunk, or spending time with other people."

"I can't just stop seeing my friends, Jack. They need me as much as you do."

"That isn't what I'm saying, Olivia. I'm saying that for a while, I think it would be good for us to just spend time together with no outside influence."

I know he's right, deep down. We really do need to focus on our relationship if we want it to work. This conversation was one I have been wanting to have for the last few weeks. As much as Jack wears his heart on his sleeve, he is the one who's most likely to bottle up how he is feeling. Perhaps I have been too hard on him. Maybe I am so focused on what has happened to me in the past that I forget about what is important: my future. *Our future.*

We spend the rest of the evening snuggled up in bed, binge-watching TV. There are so many old films on Netflix at the minute that I would have watched with my mum and sister growing up, and Jack has let me rewatch many of them. I'm not entirely sure he watched much at all as every time I looked up at him, he was just watching me, stroking my hair, and very occasionally kissing my head. I sometimes wish I could be inside his head so I can tell what he's thinking.

We are halfway through Clueless when my eyes become too heavy to stay open, and Jack stroking my hair sends me into a deep, peaceful sleep.

Jack

I don't think anyone has ever met a more damaged person than Olivia White. I vividly remember that first night we met, I was completely taken aback by her beauty. It was the beauty that sucked me in, she is a rose surrounded by thorns. She has no idea either, just how damaged she is. She doesn't see how her actions have got us here, and it is infuriating. I have no idea what films she's watched this evening because I haven't been paying attention. I have just been watching her. The way that when she smiles the corners of her ocean blue eyes crease up. The way that her nose scrunches up a little. The way she nibbles on that luscious bottom lip of hers when things start to get intense. The way she can feel emotion through a screen as if it were happening right in front of her.

I honestly believe I'm the only one that can make her a better person, and I thought I was doing just that. Until recently, that is. She has been different with me. She has been so inconsiderate of my feelings that I'm starting to think that the girl I fell in love with and the one asleep on my chest right now are two very different people. In the beginning, she would never question whether I was loyal to her or not, she would never continue pushing me until I ended up in a blind rage. Then today, I have no idea why she thinks I forced myself on her last night. Her body was practically begging for it. I only took what I was owed, what was mine to have.

Olivia White is a liar. But she is my liar. I will put up with her lies because I know no one else will. No one else has what it takes to fix her the way I can fix her. She is mine, *she will always be* mine. *She needs to step away from her toxic friends, before they ruin everything I have planned for her, for us. I won't let them poison her against me.*

As I slide out of bed to tidy up, I can't help but wonder - how can someone so breathtakingly stunning be so broken inside? Doesn't she see that the way she is acting is pushing me away? I really hope she was telling the truth earlier and that she will start trying harder. Because Olivia needs me, and I'm the only one who can save her, but only if she starts putting me first.

I wake up to the sun shining through the lodge window and the sound of birds singing. Jack is still fast asleep, so I make myself a quick coffee and sneak out onto the decking. The view is even better in the sunlight. The sun is blinding as it bounces off the lake, the water so clear that I can see the fish swimming underneath the surface. They vary in size, some no bigger than my hand and others that look like they could swallow me whole if I were to fall in. I make a mental note not to go into the lake. There must be around thirty ducks swimming on the surface, some with their babies close behind them. Well, I say babies, but they're now as big as their parents. The lake is surrounded by other lodges and trees. I didn't see anything on our way in, but from here, it looks like we might be in the middle of a forest. I take my phone out to take a quick picture of my morning view to show my mum when I'm back home. She would love this place. Her and my dad often talk about getting a campervan one day, so they can travel around the country.

I finish my coffee, taking in the view one last time before I make my way back inside our lodge. As I'm rinsing out my cup, I glance over at the man asleep in the bed. I have been so focused on my own demons that I didn't stop to think that he may have his own. He looks so peaceful when he is asleep, his hair all messy, his stubble slightly longer than he likes it. I decide to make him a coffee and leave it on the side for him whilst I take a quick bath.

Once I'm dressed in my leggings and Taylor Swift jumper, I unlock the bathroom door to find Jack making the bed. "Good morning," I say, walking up behind him. I wrap my arms around his waist.

"Good morning to you, too. Did you sleep ok?"

"I did, actually. Did you?"

He turns his body so he is facing me. "I did. What do you want to do today, Miss White?"

"Mmmm…" I really drag out the sound to make it sound like I am thinking long and hard about my decision. "I think we should go for a walk."

"A walk?" He raises a brow at me.

"Yes, a walk. I'm assuming we're surrounded by a forest, and I would like to see it."

"Well, a walk it is, then." He leans forward to peck me on the lips. "Let's leave our phones here, though. No distractions!"

"Yes, sir." I give him my best soldier salute as he takes himself into the bathroom to get ready.

I think the walk will be good for us, and I love his idea of leaving our phones here. Our generation relies on them too much. When we were children, technology was still foreign to us and now we can't live without it. Every morning when I wake up, the first thing I do is check my phone, and I hate myself for it. I remember the days when I had to sit on our family computer in the living room so everyone could see what you were doing. I would spend hours talking to my friends on MSN Messenger, which I'm not entirely sure is even still a thing. I also remember the websites I used to go on when I was slightly older, like Club Penguin and Habbo Hotel. When I think back to it now the websites were meant to be for children and teenagers, but there were definitely some creeps on there pretending to be younger than they actually were. Now, my phone is full of social media apps, which have been so detrimental for my mental health. It took me a while to realise that what people post online is only a small part of their life, and it isn't realistic. Nobody's life is as perfect as it appears online. Maybe we should normalise posting real life instead of these snippets of perfection.

Chapter 13

The walk was amazing, spending time just the two of us, climbing trees like big children. I did get stuck once. No, that's a lie. I got stuck three times. Jack saved me every time. I used to love spending time in the forest by my friend's house when I was little. We used to build dens and traps and try to catch all kinds of wildlife. Today reminded me of that fun. We walked for four hours in total, talking about life and what our idea of a perfect future together would be. We decided we would like two children, to still live in town to be close to both of our families, and to buy a house with four bedrooms, one would be used as a home office/homework room, and we would have cats.

We always had cats growing up and I have always preferred them to dogs, though I am aware that's an unpopular opinion. Our mum got Rose and I each a kitten. I was just going into year eight at school, so I was at the height of being bullied when we brought him home, and he saved my life. Most people think I'm crazy when I tell them the story, but he made me feel like I had a purpose. Whenever I'm upset, he comes to find me and lies with me. He was a friend to me when I had nobody else to turn to. I could talk to him and tell him all my problems, but he couldn't say a word back to me. He has loved me through it all. I named him Terrence. I never have been able to name my pets the usual names like Rose did as a child, I always give them what I would consider "human names." Even my hamsters were called Ant and Dec.

Sitting in the hot tub, we are looking out towards the lake. Jack was kind enough to lend me one of his shirts to wear so I felt more comfortable. I have tried my hardest to accept my body and love the way I look, but after years of bullying and abuse from different men, I don't think I will ever be comfortable naked. I also want to keep the bruises on my body as covered as possible, so I don't have to keep reliving what happened the other night. We each have a glass of wine, white for me and red for him. Jack is much more comfortable than I am and has opted to wear just his boxers. I'm not complaining, though, because it allows me to drool over his toned arms and shoulders. He still has a slight tan left over from the summer heat, which leaves him looking bronzed.

"I had fun today," I say to him across the tub.

"Me too. We should come away more often. It's nice when it's just the two of us."

"I'm not sure Cindy would let me have all of that time off."

"Well, then maybe you should look for another job. I don't like you working there anyway."

My brows pull together. "You don't?"

"No Liv. I've seen some of the people that go into that shop, the type of people that steal whatever they can get their hands on to sell, just so they can afford their next fix."

I know what he's on about, we do have the occasional person come in who steals our most expensive items. We were told by the head office not to approach them and to let them take whatever they wanted. It isn't safe for us to try to intervene. We always call the police after and hand them a copy of the CCTV so they can investigate it themselves, but most of the time nothing ever comes from it.

"I have worked really hard to get where I am, Jack. I can't just give it all up now."

"You could find a safer job," he clears his throat, "you don't need to work anyway, I earn enough to look after us both."

A long sigh leaves my body as I move over to his side of the hot tub and take his head in my hands. "I appreciate it, Jack, trust me, I really do, but... I need to do this. I have to do this for myself."

He kisses my palm. "Just consider it. Please."

"Ok."

"I hate that I did this to you," he says, eyeing the bruises on my wrists. "I'll stop taking it, Liv. I don't want to do this to you again."

"It isn't your fault that this happened. I know you would never hurt me on purpose."

"You can't tell anyone, Olivia," he looks deep into my eyes, "if you tell, they'll arrest me."

"I would never put you in that position. You know that. I love you."

"I love you too."

We spend the rest of the evening sat in the tub. Jack uses his phone to get us some dinner delivered instead of him having to drive to the nearest town and find something for us both. We each finish a bottle of wine, which I know I will regret in the morning. We go to bed in the early hours of the morning after watching some TV. Tonight, I let Jack pick what films he wanted to watch as I got the feeling he didn't enjoy the ones I picked last night.

This morning it's raining, so we're stuck inside. Jack was up before me, and he had a coffee waiting for me. I bought a book with me just in case the weather did turn bad. I rummage through my bag to find the new novel by Paisley Hope as Jack sits scrolling through TikTok on his phone.

Rose and I have the same taste in books, if there's no smut in it, we probably won't read it. She got me hooked on Elsie Silver's Chestnut Spring series, and since then, I have been a sucker for a cowboy romance.

I find when I'm reading, it helps me escape from reality, I can focus purely on the words in front of me and forget the noise in my head. It silences my brain in a way that no kind of therapy or medication ever has. Unless you read, I don't think you understand how it can make someone feel. Since I have been with Jack, I haven't read as much. He thinks it's weird and a waste of time. I have tried explaining that it is exactly the same as when he plays his PlayStation, that you become engrossed in another universe, but he tells me it's different. I have an Amazon Wishlist full of the books I would like to buy. There is probably enough for me to start my own library, but I hardly ever buy them because I can't handle another argument with him about how I'm wasting my money. The one I am reading at the moment I got from work. I got it on my lunch break when Jack was not there to tell me no.

"Did you buy another book?" He asks, looking at me over the top of his phone.

"No." I say too quickly. "I borrowed this one from Louise."

Louise and I have been friends for a few days longer than me and Lily have. We met on the induction day you have before you start upper school, and then we were in the same form class for the rest of our school lives. We even went to Sixth Form together before I failed. We have been to a number of different concerts over the years: Taylor Swift, 30 Seconds to Mars, You Me at Six, Enter Shikari, and All Time Low.

I am two entirely different people. There is one who is girly and loves all things makeup, clothes, romance, and Taylor Swift. Then the other one is all band tees, vans, gigs, and You Me at Six. It really depends on the mood I'm in when I wake up in the morning.

Louise and I lost touch for a while. Life got in the way until Taylor Swift released her UK Era's Tour dates. We then decided we would go together as we did on her Red Tour years ago, and we've stayed in touch ever since. Even though we hadn't seen each other for a good few years, it felt like we had never been apart.

"When did you get time to see her?"

"She came into work the other day to buy some new books, and she bought it with her because she thought I would like it." I lie.

"She just happened to know you were working, did she?"

"No. It was a lucky guess. She knows I work there, and she was hoping I would be there that day. Even if I wasn't working, she was going to leave it behind the till for me."

Louise is more of a fantasy reader than she is a romance reader, but Jack doesn't know that. Nor does he need to.

He rolls his eyes at me before turning his attention back to his phone. I spend all of my spare time with Jack. Some days he even comes and hangs out in the shop whilst I'm working, so he knows I wouldn't have had time to meet her outside of working hours. I'm not sure if he can tell I am lying or not. There was a time when he wouldn't follow me everywhere I went. Now, though, I can't even go to the toilet without him asking where I'm going. If my phone goes off, he likes to know who is messaging me and why. It has got a bit too much for me, but I don't tell him that. I don't want to upset him.

Chapter 14

The rest of the day goes by in a blur. I get through a good chunk of my book, and then Jack decides it would be easier for us to travel home tonight instead of tomorrow morning. I know he's probably right. Neither of us are morning people, and we're likely to sleep in and miss the checking out window. But I also wonder if it's because I upset him earlier. I never have been a good liar.

I pack up our bags, and he takes them out to the car when I'm done. This time away has been incredible. We have spent so much quality time together, and it feels like it did when we first got together. I'll miss our tiny wooden home, but I cannot wait to get back and organise a night with my favourite girls.

"This is the last of it," I say to him, handing him the final bag before turning to lock the door one final time.

"Thank you," he mumbles, "what are you going to do with the rest of your week off?"

"Well, as you're off as well, I was hoping we could spend it together, maybe do some Christmas shopping."

"No, I'm going to go back to work. I want to save my holiday."

My brows pull together. He told me today that he was looking forward to spending the rest of the week together. I shake away the horrible thoughts that come into my mind and get into the car silently. I use this time to update my friends on my whereabouts and to tell my mum that we'll be home tonight instead of tomorrow. Jack joins me in the car, punching my address into his map app and with that, we start our journey home.

“Do you want me to put some music on?” I ask him. The silence suddenly feels heavy.

“Yes.” I reach for his phone because I know he won’t enjoy the unpredictability of my playlists. Hopefully, his music might lighten the mood a little bit. “Use your phone, Olivia. I don’t want you going through mine.”

I cock my head and frown at him in the darkness. Why would I go through his phone? Does he have something to hide? We haven’t even made it out of the lodge site yet and he’s already back to how he has been.

“Ok, but please don’t complain about what comes on then,” I say to him. We talked about a lot of things this weekend, but one of the key issues he had was me pushing him, so I let the tone of his voice, and his secretiveness go. I hit shuffle, and a text from my mum comes through.

Mum: Ok, tell Jack to drive safely. We won’t be at home tonight, we’re about to drive over to Nans.

Me: Is everything ok?

Mum: I am not sure yet, but I will let you know. Love you xx

My nan lives on her own. Our grandad died when we were little. She refuses to move out of their big semi-detached three-bedroom house, which means we have to drive a good thirty minutes to her house if she needs us.

“Mum and Dad won’t be home tonight when we get back, by the way. They had to drive over to my nans.” I inform Jack.

“Why?”

“She hasn’t said yet, but she said she would update me when she knows more.”

He reaches his hand across the car and squeezes my thigh tightly. “Everything will be ok, Liv.”

“You don’t know that.”

“Hey, enough of that. She’s a strong woman. She can overcome anything that’s thrown her way.”

I close my eyes and sleep for the rest of the drive home to stop myself from thinking about the worst things possible. I dream about my family, a Christmas eve at my nans house. Rose and I stayed over the night with my mum and uncle. We had KFC for dinner and tracked Santa on the computer. We had been in bed for a while, but I was thirsty, so I got up to get myself a drink. I got halfway down the stairs, and I caught my mum and nan pulling wrapped Christmas presents out of an old Argos bag. I still believed in Santa until that night, but I didn't tell them I had caught them. I still don't think I have told my mum to this day that I don't believe anymore.

Jack wakes me when we pull up outside my parents' house. "Come on, baby, we're home."

I unbuckle my seatbelt and get out of the car. Whilst I am waiting for Jack to get our bags, I check my phone to see if I have received any news from my mum. I haven't but I have got one from Rose.

Rose: Have you heard from Mum yet?

Me: No. She told me she was heading out there, but I haven't heard anything back from her yet.

Rose: Ok. Same here.

Rose: I'm going to go to sleep. Let me know if you hear from her.

Me: Will do. I love you x

Rose: I love you too, Livvy Lu x

By the time we are in bed, I'm full of anxiety. My mum would be there by now. Jack pulls me to his chest and strokes my hair to try and settle me. He texted his boss earlier to tell him he would be back at work tomorrow morning, so I know I can't keep him up. It wouldn't be fair for him to have to go in tired because I've managed to get myself worked up. He told me I needed to start taking his feelings into consideration, so I just lay here on his chest in silence, staring at the wall, listening just in case my phone goes off. I'm not entirely sure how long I manage to stay awake before I fall asleep, but when I wake up, the sun is up, and Jack is gone.

I roll over to check my phone and see my mum has texted me, but I can't bring myself to open it just yet. Instead, I open the message from Jack.

Jack: Morning, beautiful. I hope I didn't wake you when I left this morning. Let me know if you hear anything from your mum. I need to go home after I finish work, but I will come to yours after.

Before I message him back, I brave it and check the message from my mum so I can give him the update he wants.

Mum: Nan is in hospital. I will be coming home this morning to shower, and then you can come back up with me. She is stable and conscious.

I feel relief and dread at the same time. Relief that she is ok and is getting the help she clearly needs, but dread because something has obviously happened, and it must be bad for her to have to stay in hospital.

I quickly fire Jack a text to let him know what is going on and I let him know that I will be going up with my mum. He has a key to our house now because of how often he's here, so he will be able to let himself in when he's finished doing whatever he needs to do at his parents' house.

As I finish drying my hair, I hear my mum and dad downstairs. I quickly throw on a pair of black cycling shorts and a Guns N' Roses T-shirt before leaving my room to find them. My mum looks tired. That is my first thought when I see her. I can tell she has been up all night. My dad doesn't look much better. He gives me a small smile as he passes me to go upstairs to freshen up.

"Mum?" I ask, anxiously waiting for the blow that I know will quickly follow.

She takes a deep breath in, tears already filling her eyes. "She will be fine. She had a stroke, but it was a mini one."

The world around me freezes.

My nan is the strongest, most independent woman I know. She is known for her killer roast dinners and her gardening skills. She is the woman who still slides us money for the ice cream van, new clothes, and nights out even though we're all grown up and have our own jobs. She is the head of this family, and I can't imagine a world where that changes.

The tears are flowing from my eyes as my mum takes me into her arms. I didn't even think about how this would make her feel. She may be my nan, but that is her mother. The very idea of something like this happening to my mum makes me sick to my stomach.

"Do they know how bad it is?" I manage to get out between sobs.

"She still has full movement. It is a little weaker on her left side, but she can move, eat, and speak." My mum reassures me. "Let me call Rose and get myself ready, and we can all head over there."

I let her go. Rose has always been closer to our nan than I have. If it has hit me this hard, it will destroy her. I was a grandad's girl growing up. Regardless of how much time has passed, it never gets easier for me to accept that he is gone. He was the first man to make me feel safe and wanted, it wasn't his job to do those things, but he didn't care. He was so proud of us girls, we were his entire world.

When we would drive over for Sunday dinner, he would be asleep after his night shift. By the time Nan would have dinner ready we would be itching to run upstairs to wake him up. We had to wait for permission, though. When it was given, we would run like Usain Bolt up those stairs and burst into their bedroom. We used to think we were being so quiet as we crept across the room and climbed onto the bed. Then we would jump and scream until he woke up. Years after he passed, our mum told us he was never really asleep, he would just pretend for us. He was taken from us far too soon, and he left a massive hole in all of our hearts.

I follow my mum up the stairs to finish getting ready myself whilst she calls Rose and sorts herself out.

All I manage to do is pull my hair up into a ponytail and apply some moisturiser. I know the second I see her in that hospital bed, I will crumble, so there really is no need for makeup. It would just be a waste.

We head to Rose's before we set off for the hospital, which is an hour away from here. We have already popped into the local supermarket to grab a few of my nan's favourite things. She would live on a diet of Maltesers if we let her, so we grabbed a few bags of those as well as some of her favourite magazines, a few word-search books we're hoping she hasn't already done, and some grapes. My mum already stopped by my nans on the way back home to grab the essentials she will need over the next few days.

As Rose approaches our mum's car, I hop out of the front seat and get in the back. Since she has been pregnant, she has been extremely travel-sick unless she is sitting in the front, and I do not fancy being covered in vomit. When we're all buckled in, my mum starts the car again and starts the long drive to the hospital.

"Prepare yourselves, girls. She will be ok, but she doesn't look her best. Try not to look around the ward either."

Chapter 15

She's sleeping when we arrive, and Rose and I tell our mum not to wake her. We will wait until she wakes up to speak to her.

She looks so small, and it hits me hard as I see her for the first time. So fragile and vulnerable. Laid there hooked up to a number of different machines. Her face seems hollow and her silver hair lies flat against her forehead. It's such a shock to see her in this state. She is usually so full of life and personality. As she is on a stroke ward, everyone here is in the same position that she is. The main ward is separated into smaller wards. She's in a section with other patients who have had the same level of stroke that she has had, the less severe type, if there is such a thing.

As we sit here beside her a nurse comes around and asks if it's ok to close the curtains that separate the beds. We say yes, and then she makes her way down the beds, asking the same question to the other patients. For a few moments, there is silence. And then, from afar, the noise of a bed being rolled through the main ward grows louder. With the curtains drawn, the events remain unseen, but the distant cries and the quiet demeanor of the staff throughout the ward make it easy to piece everything together.

I look back at my nan, realising how lucky we are that she is still here with us. It doesn't matter to me how different she may be now all of this has happened as long as she is here. As a family, we will help her in any way that we can so she can get back to her normal life.

Nan wakes up when my mum is off looking for a doctor to get an update on her condition. I find her glasses on the unit beside her bed and hand them to her. Her eyes are tired and vacant, but she still smiles at us both.

"If you wanted us to come and see you, you only had to call, you know," I say to her.

Humour is my way of coping with tricky situations. Not everyone understands that, but my nan appreciates it. I can tell because the smile on her face grows bigger and brighter. She would much rather us continue as if everything were normal, as she absolutely hates when people try to take care of her.

She lets out a small chuckle before eyeing up the carrier bag at the foot of her bed. "What did you bring me?" Her voice is raspy.

"We got you magazines, word-search books and chocolate," I say, handing the bag to her. "We did also pick up some grapes so when the doctors come around you can at least pretend to be healthy."

"Oh, awake now, are we?" My mum says from behind me. "What's this I hear about you refusing to get out of bed?"

My nan glares at her only daughter like she just murdered a puppy right in front of her. I should also say my mum was a daddy's girl. She believes my nan's favourite child is my uncle.

"I was tired," my nan says to her as she tears open her first bag of Maltesers.

"Why don't we try and get you up now? See if you can walk to the toilet to freshen up."

"I don't want to."

I pride myself on being stubborn. I get my stubbornness from my mum, and my mum gets it from my nan. I know my mum is more stubborn than I am, but with these two, I think they are tied. It's always fun to sit back and watch them, you can never guess which one will cave first. Today, my mum doesn't even try to argue with her. I think the fact my nan is in a hospital bed wins.

"How are you feeling, Nan?" Rose asks.

"Fine, but they keep stabbing me with needles and prodding me."

"They just want to make sure you get the help you need. It's only for a few days, and then you will be home again. It will be like none of this happened." I'm not sure if she says this more to herself than she does to our nan.

"Well, I am fine." My nan says.

"You are not fine, Mum. You had a stroke." My mum rolls her eyes at my nan.

"A mini one," she adds back.

"A stroke is a stroke." My mum says before adding, "You will be here until they think you are fit enough to go home. If they ask you to do something, then do it. If you put the effort in and they can see you're able to look after yourself, then you'll be allowed home quicker."

We stay sitting with her for a few more hours. She does, in fact, get up and go to the toilet when one of the nurses asks her. They have planned for the Physiotherapy team to come around and assess her. She will likely be in here for the rest of the week whilst they make sure she recovers properly. My nan doesn't like the idea of that at all. She hates hospitals and much prefers being at home, sat on the sofa watching TV. We did try to tell her that this is good news and that she will be home in time for Christmas. When she started getting sleepy again, we decided to leave and let her get the rest her body so desperately needed.

Now, we are all piled back in the car and are on our way home. The first half of the journey is silent. I have been sitting in the back thinking about the time we spent with her today, how precious life is and how quickly it can be taken away from you. She is not the healthiest woman I have ever met, but she is also not unhealthy. The hospital staff will tell her to stop smoking, but we all know she will never do such a thing. Yet again, she is a stubborn woman, and if she doesn't want to do something, she simply will not do it.

"It was nice to see her," I say from the back. "She looked better than I thought she would."

"She will be fine as long as she listens to what they say," Mum eyes me in the rearview mirror.

"She won't do anything she doesn't want to do. You know how she is."

"Well, she won't have a choice. If she wants to get better, then she needs to do the work."

We all know it's true.

When we arrive home after dropping Rose off, I notice Jack isn't here. I pull my phone out to send him a text message. It isn't like him to just not show up. If he's running late or can't make it, he always tells me. The last time I heard from him was when we were still at the hospital, when I updated him and told him what had happened. He sent his love, and then I told him I was on my way home, and I haven't heard anything since.

I choose to treat myself to a soothing, warm bubble bath to cleanse away the stress of the day. I often feel dirty after returning from the hospital. As the bath fills up, I pick up my book, light several candles, and make a large mug of tea. This kind of bath is my absolute favourite. It's the perfect opportunity for me to completely unwind and relax.

My phone buzzes, and I pick it up to see if it's Jack.

Nat: I'm on my way to work, and I swear I just saw your boyfriend sat in the pub?

Me: Really? I haven't heard from him in a few hours. I was up at the hospital seeing my nan.

Nat: He was with one of those girls you usually come in the club with and a boy, I think.

Nat: Hope your nan is doing better!

Me: It could be Jordan or Dylan. Thank you for letting me know. She will be ok. The worst is over now, I think.

Nat: Your family are tough as nails. She will be fine. What about the girl?

Me: That's true. It could be Daisy or Georgia. It's more likely Georgia if Jordan is there.

Nat: Let me know when you find out. I know the perfect place to bury a body.

I try to call Jack. He probably just got carried away talking to our friends and lost track of time. The call goes to voicemail, but I don't stress over it because I know where he is and who he is with. I'm thankful to Nat for telling me because otherwise, I would've started going out of my mind with worry.

I turn my ponytail into a bun and step into the bath. If having a bath was an Olympic sport, I would win gold every single time. In fact, I would live in the bath if I could. Usually, I have Taylor Swift turned up on full volume and sing my little head off like it's my own personal concert. Jack doesn't like it when I sing, so those bath concerts have become a rare occurrence. After half an hour, my fingers are shrivelled from the water, and my stomach is screaming at me to eat, so I get out.

When I get downstairs, I order some dinner for me and my parents. We chose kebabs because who doesn't like a good kebab? We start talking about Christmas plans as Jack and I weren't together last year, and my parents would like to know where I will be spending the day.

"I'll be here," I say, "I could never spend Christmas away from you both. Jack knows that and he said he will come up here in the evening after he's had Christmas dinner with his family."

"You will struggle, you know?" My mum adds. "Both of you value spending time with your family. Sooner or later, you will have to decide where you want to spend the day as a couple."

A big sigh leaves me as I pull my knees to my chest on the sofa. "I know that, but I couldn't imagine not spending the day with all of you."

"Well, obviously, I would prefer to see you for at least part of the day, but Jack also has a family he loves and would like to see."

"It's sorted for this year anyway. Next year is next year's problem. We will both spend time with our own families, and he will come here after."

We have had many conversations around Christmas since we've been together. My mum is right. Neither of us wants to spend the day away from the people we love, but we also want to spend the time together. I always imagined when I was older that, I would bring my children over to my parent's house, and we would all have Christmas dinner together. This is probably another example of me not taking other people's feelings into consideration and just thinking of myself. Jack told me as much the other day. Next year, we will have to have a better plan on how we will spend Christmas. We will probably be living together by then, so we won't be able to avoid it for much longer. I just can't imagine spending the day away from my mum and sister.

This Christmas will be different already, because of my nan not being well. The likelihood is she will not be able to help with the Christmas dinners anymore. I'm trying not to think about what the effects of her stroke could be, but I can't seem to help it. After seeing her so fragile and a shell of herself today, I think she has changed. Maybe she seems okay on the outside but on the inside, it is bound to leave scars.

We eat our dinner and continue having conversations about what to get each other well into the late evening. Since Rose has been pregnant, there's been a lot of talk about us all doing a Secret Santa going forward. This may very well be the last Christmas we have together as a family where we can really spoil each other, so I want to make sure I get everyone the perfect gift. When I go up to bed, I check my phone again and I still haven't heard back from Jack. My screen is filled with messages I have sent him, but he hasn't even opened them.

Me: We're on our way back now. We will have to drop Rose off but then I am all yours.

Me: I'm just going to have a bath then I will order dinner. Would you like anything?

Me: Mum and Dad were hungry, so I had to order. I love you x

Me: Is everything ok? Nat said she saw you in the pub. Did you forget the time?

Me: Have I done something to upset you?

Me: I'm going to bed now. I will leave my phone on loud in case you call. I love you.

I do as I said and leave my phone on loud under my pillow. If he is with his brother, then he's probably just got sidetracked and coming over must have slipped his mind. He has to be up for work in the morning, so I know he will either go home or come here soon. I close my eyes and cuddle up to Jack's pillow. There is a slight hint of his aftershave, which makes me feel cosier.

Chapter 16

It's still dark when I'm woken up by my phone ringing. I quickly turn it on silent, so it doesn't wake anyone else up, and I answer it.

"Hello"

"About time. I'm outside. You going to let me in or not?"

"You have a key, Jack."

"I know I have a key, Olivia. But some idiots put the chain on the door."

"That would be my mum. She isn't an idiot, she just didn't know if you were coming over or not."

"Obviously, I am. All of my stuff is here."

"Well, you didn't text me back, so I couldn't tell her if you were staying or not."

"Because you were selfish and only thought about yourself again. Are you going to open this door or not? If not, then I will start knocking and you can explain to your mum why you thought it was ok to not let me in tonight." He hangs up the phone.

I roll over and get out of bed, checking the time before I make my way downstairs to let him in. It's one in the morning. *Where has he been?* The pubs in town closed over two hours ago now. I know this because there have been many nights where I have sat down there with him until we were kicked out at closing time.

My friends and I have never been massive drinkers. We go on the occasional night out to let our hair down, but the midweek drinking is a new thing. Jack drinks daily, whether that's at home or down the pub, he isn't fussy. Initially, it was nice to be out in public with him, I had never had anyone want to show me off the way he does, but eventually, it got too much for me. It just isn't what I want for my own life. If I'm being totally honest, I can't stand drunk people. It brings back a lot of memories from my childhood that I would like to forget.

We have spoken about it and Jack said he understood and that he would stop going as well because he wanted to spend time with me, and initially he did, but then he started going again. I haven't mentioned it to him since, because if it's what he wants to spend his free time doing then that is up to him.

I take the chain off the front door and open it for him. He's still dressed in the clothes he wore to work today. A pair of worn grey jogging bottoms and a muscle-fit white T-shirt. Work Jack is another of my favourite looks on him, not my most favourite but it's definitely still a nice sight. I let my eyes roam their way up his toned body until they land on his face, and then my heart stops beating.

"Don't start, Olivia. I'm not in the mood." Jack pushes past me and makes his way upstairs to my room.

Why would he do this? What have I done?

I stand there for a moment in utter disbelief. After composing myself and locking the front door, I make my way up to my room to find him already laid in my bed. I'm too shocked to speak, so I just get into bed beside him and turn my back to him. I know now exactly where he has been and what he has been doing. His eyes are once again foreign to me. He promised me he would try to stop. He said he would do it for us. *Are we not worth fighting for?*

He sighs into the darkness before he speaks, "I told you to start thinking about my feelings, Olivia. Please tell me when you have thought about me today?"

"I don't want to do this right now, Jack. Please. Just go to sleep, and we can talk about it tomorrow."

"I am not waiting till tomorrow for you to apologise to me. We will talk about this now!"

I say nothing. I just stare at my wall through the darkness. Apologise for what? Apologise for spending the day with my sick nan? The evening with my family? I kept him updated. I told him everything I was doing and when I was doing it.

"You really need me to spell it out to you, Liv?" He says, breaking the silence. "You really thought I was going to come here whilst you were out with your mum and sister? You thought I would just sit here and wait for you? No, Olivia. That will never happen. You really think you're special, don't you? You think you are better than everyone else? News flash, you're not! You are nothing without me. You should be thanking me for putting up with you and the mess that you are. It's always about what you want and how you feel. You still don't think about me and what I want and need. I told you we need to spend more time together. Instead, you chose to sit up a hospital."

"What are you talking about? You think I had fun today?" I sit up in my bed and turn to him. "You think I enjoyed seeing my nan in that state? She needs her family around her, Jack. I will not apologise for wanting to help her through this."

"I should come first, Olivia. Me. Our relationship should come before anyone else."

He cannot be serious right now. He knows how much my family means to me. Is he right, though? I did just expect him to be here when I got home, and I am nothing without him. Without him, I'm just a damaged girl who doesn't know where her place is in this world. But if he thinks we need to spend more time together then why did he spend all night down the pub? Why did he take drugs again when he knows how I feel about it?

"Why did you take the drugs, Jack?"

"Because you pushed me again, Olivia. You forgot about everything we spoke about when we were away. You went straight back to thinking about yourself and no one else. Daisy and Dylan wanted to spend time with me. They think you're selfish as well by the way. Daisy told me to go home tonight, she told me I shouldn't even bother explaining myself to you, but I still came, because I love you. If you loved me you would've been here waiting for me when I finished work."

"You spoke to our friends about this?"

"My friends Olivia. Mine."

"What do you want me to say, Jack?"

He sighs. "I want you to apologise to me, and then I want you to give me what you haven't been giving me lately, because you claim I raped you."

I run my fingers through my hair before bowing my head into my hands. I can't pinpoint when the tears began to fall, but they are now streaming into my palms. I'm utterly bewildered. It feels as though I am on the brink of losing my sanity. I believed I was doing better, that I was considering how my actions would impact him. I have no desire to argue with him. I can't afford to lose him. I despise the person I was before Jack came into my life, a girl who was afraid of her own shadow. He is exactly what I need. I am certain of that. He has the ability to care for me in ways that no one else can.

"I'm sorry," I say into my hands. "I am so sorry, ok. I have had a really rubbish day, and yes, I probably didn't think about you as much as I should've."

"That wasn't hard, was it? Now come here."

He reaches for me, and I know what's coming next, but I don't want to. I am so ashamed of myself. Embarrassed even. I don't want him to touch me.

"I don't want to Jack. I just want to sleep."

"You owe me, Olivia. You will give me what you owe me."

"Stop, Jack. I don't want to, not today!"

"Don't be so selfish. This is how you make it up to me. How you make things right again."

Before I can protest further, he has his hands on me. He lays me face down on the bed, my hands under my chest so I cannot move. He pulls my hair from my face and gathers it up into a ponytail. I'm not strong enough to fight him off, so I don't even try. I am too tired, both mentally and physically. I just let him take what he wants from me. I am nothing. Just a poison that doesn't deserve any shred of happiness

Chapter 17

The rest of the week goes by painfully slow. I barely move from my bed. I live my life minimally. I do just enough so my parents don't ask questions that I'm not ready to answer. Jack has been here and when he has told me to eat and bathe, I have done so. I'm meant to go out with Lily and Natalia tonight, but I have no idea what I'm meant to say to them. I think I will probably just lie and say I'm ok and hope that they believe it. I've been rather good at hiding how bad I feel on the inside for my entire life. I am still so ashamed of myself. I have apologised an endless number of times to Jack, and he says it's ok, but I know deep down it isn't. He deserves to be with someone who can give him the world, and that person is not me right now.

I have curled my hair and styled it in a half-up, half-down hairstyle. My makeup is the best I've had it in the last year. I have gone with my usual look, winged liner, and a red lip, but I finally managed to find a contour shade that works for my porcelain skin. As I am not feeling my best, I have opted for a pair of black skinny jeans and a low-cut, scalloped white bodysuit. Usually, I get my legs out any chance I can, so I'm hoping that Lily and Natalia fail to pick up on the fact I am more covered than usual. I look so put together on the outside, which means stage one of my "act ok" plan has gone well.

I down my glass of cheap wine and refill it as Jack comes into my room. He said he would stay here tonight, and when I'm ready to come home, he will come down and meet me. He's going to watch the football with my dad to pass the time.

"Is that what you're going to wear?" He asks, with a brow raised.

"I am indeed. I thought it was still dressy enough to look nice, but-"

"That top is a little low, don't you think?" He cuts me off.

"I don't think so. It covers everywhere that needs covering, and it's more reserved than a lot of other things I own."

"Change it, Olivia." He turns and leaves my room.

I roll my eyes and let out a sigh as I look at myself in the mirror. It is a little low. Maybe he doesn't want other men to get the wrong idea. I quickly rummage through my wardrobe for a top that is slightly more reserved. I opt for a high-neck black bodysuit. The only skin showing now is from my shoulders to my fingertips.

I say my goodbyes to my family and Jack and start the walk to town. He approved of my outfit change and honestly, I feel more comfortable like this anyway. The town is heaving. There are many groups of people that are out for their work Christmas parties. The women are dressed in sequins, and the men are in their three-piece suits, which is unusual to see in this tiny town.

As I walk to the front door of our usual pub, I find Natalia waiting for me. She looks incredible. She is also wearing a pair of skinny jeans. Hers are a shade of deep blue. She has paired them with a V-neck white cropped top. She is so naturally beautiful. Her chestnut brown hair is straightened, and it flows down to her waist. Like Lily, she wears minimal makeup, just a little mascara, which shows off how ridiculously long her eyelashes are, and a nude pink lipstick on her lips. Every time I see her, I'm sure her eyes have changed colour. I'm still undecided if they are blue, grey, or even green. Either way, they are stunning.

"I didn't realise we were partying with a nun tonight," she says when she sees me.

This makes me fire her a smile. "Haha, very funny. We are basically wearing the same thing, so I could say the same to you."

"No, babe, we are not. My cleavage is out. You left yours at home."

I hug my best friend, she's not a hugger, so she just hovers there awkwardly until I pull away from her. "I don't have a cleavage anyway. I missed you bitch!"

“Do not ever hug me again,” she says back to me as she takes my hand in hers and leads me into the pub.

Lily arrives by the time we have found a table to sit at. The group chat was full of messages about the two of them going shopping for something new and dressy to wear and yet they are both wearing basically the same thing. The only difference is that Lily’s top is off-the-shoulder with long sleeves. It isn’t long before we have all consumed two glasses of wine and are oversharing.

It has been bliss, sitting here with two of my favourite people on this earth, catching up on every detail in each other's lives. Lily has been telling us about her job as a teacher. She was made to work with children. One day, she will make the best mother. She puts her all into her job, and when she talks about it, you can see the love for it shine in her eyes. Natalia has been with her boyfriend for five years. He lives four hours away, but they have made it work until now. She’s become fed up with the way he treats her. He cheats on her constantly and degrades her daily. We have told her several times to leave. She has such a big bright personality, that she deserves to be with a person who will let her shine. She’s so loyal and has so much love to give it’s a shame she wastes it all on someone who doesn’t appreciate her.

When it gets to me, I tell them how I have been struggling. My nan is getting stronger with every day that passes. She should be discharged over the next few days. I say how I have been unfair to Jack. How I have been taking him for granted and I promised that I will try better. I tell them how my sister will be having her baby soon after Christmas. I tell them everything because I can.

They are my second family; they make me feel safe and heard. We are there for each other through the thick and the thin. We keep each other from falling apart. For the first time this week, I feel happy. I’m not having to pretend.

“Wait a minute. *You* are going to try to be better?” Nat looks disgusted.

“Yes. He wants us to spend more time together. He thinks I don’t appreciate him.”

"That is bullshit." I glare at her. "Sorry, Liv, but you do everything he tells you to."

"If that was true Nat then we wouldn't be having the problems we are."

Lily takes my hand in hers, "I know you, Liv. We both do. There is no way that you are the problem. You have the kindest soul."

Nat chokes on her drink before adding, "What she said. But maybe worded differently."

"There is nothing wrong with expressing your emotions, Natalia Taylor."

"Do not full name me, Lily Jones."

I take my hand back from Lily to top up everyone's glasses with the last of the wine.

"Both of you are such children. You know that, right?"

"Just be careful, Liv. You don't owe him anything. Men are pigs." Nat says before chugging her wine.

"Are you sure you're not just projecting?" I raise an eyebrow at her.

As we are leaving the pub to head to the club, I pull my phone out to check on how Jack's evening is going, but he has already been blowing my phone up.

Jack: Make sure you don't drink too much.

Jack: Your mum said you need to be safe as I'm not there.

Jack: Olivia?

Jack: Are you serious right now?

Jack: This is the last time you will be going out with your friends if you're not going to respond. You are so selfish and irresponsible.

I freeze in the street, staring at my phone. I have only been gone for three hours, and he is already acting like this.

Me: My phone has been in my bag. We've been busy catching up on life and having fun. Heading to the club now.

When I lift my head up the drink hits me, and it makes me laugh to myself. I put my phone back in my bag and catch up with my friends.

"Have you seen the new bouncer?" Nat says as I link one arm with her and one with Lily.

"No, I can't say I have. Why?" I ask her

She lets out a deep laugh after she says what sounds like "yum."

"I could never date a bouncer. Imagine how many girls hit on them every night!" Lily gets out around her laugh.

"You won't say that when you see him, Lil. I promise you that. I would climb him like a tree if I was single," Nat adds.

"No. I think Lily has a point, Nat."

Lily is definitely the mum of our group. She still knows how to have fun, but she has always been more sensible than me and Nat are. She rounds us up at the end of the night and makes sure we both get home safe.

As we round the corner, the club comes into view, and we all freeze. "Wow," I manage to get out. "Ok. I take it back. Lily your point is invalid."

This man is beautiful. He has short blonde hair, which I don't usually find attractive. I can see his million-dollar smile from here. His white teeth shine brightly against his all-black uniform. What woman doesn't like a man in uniform?

"Wait till you hear him speak," Nat says as she wriggles her arm free and walks ahead. Her working here has its benefits. If we are ever out with her, they let us all in free of charge, and the night is usually spent consuming way too many free drinks. "Hello, trouble."

"You're even here on your night off?" The bouncer asks in a deep and thick Birmingham accent. I'm pretty sure it's an accent people used to find annoying until Tommy Shelby came along, and now I can't find a single woman my age that finds it unattractive.

I have died and gone to heaven. My jaw is dragging on the floor by the time we catch up to her. He isn't the tallest man in the world, but height has never bothered me when it comes to men. I don't understand why there is such a stigma about a man having to be taller than a woman. Why does it matter? I can reach the top shelf for him.

His eyes find mine, and I'm taken back by them. My eyes are the bluest eyes I have ever seen, at least until the moment that this man looked into my soul with his. They are as blue as the sky on a clear summer's day. Blue eyes and blonde hair are not on the list of things I look for when I date a man, so it must be the uniform.

"I hope you two are not liabilities like your friend here is," he says.

Lily nudges me to urge me to speak "Worse." That's all that leaves my mouth.

I quickly pull myself together and follow Nat into the club. Jack would lose his mind if he saw me right now. It isn't long until we are all on the dance floor with a drink in each hand. It's still early, so the club isn't too busy. We have all the space we need to dance like our lives depend on it. The bouncers in the club swap place every twenty or so minutes, alternating between the dance floor and the main door, so I know I will see McDreamy again before the night is over. Our towns very own blonde version of Derek Shepherd. I would never touch another man whilst I'm in a relationship, but I can appreciate a good-looking man when I see one.

We are just about to grab our next drink when Low by Flo Rida comes on, and we all go feral. It isn't a song I would actively go out of my way to listen to when I'm sober, but when I have had a drink, there is nothing I love more. The club is busier now, but we still have room to get low, and we do. I'm too busy twerking on Nat to notice McDreamy has swapped positions. When I look up at Lily, her eyes are bulging from her head, so I look over my shoulder and there he is, watching us with a smile on his face. I turn back to Lily, who is now doubled over laughing. As the song changes, I drag them both to the nearest bar. My cheeks hurt where I have been laughing and smiling with them so much.

"I love you both. You know that, right?" I shout over the music

"We love you too," they say in unison

“I never want us to lose this.” I pout at them.

“Take your shot and drink, you soppy mess,” Nat shouts back at me. “What is wrong with both of you tonight. Too emotional for me.”

“But we love you so much Nat!” Lily shouts at her as she grabs her face in her hands and gives her forehead a big sloppy kiss.

I am so grateful for these women. Each of us has been through our own fair share of troubles, and maybe that’s what makes us so close. The ability to understand how the others are feeling. All I know is I will not lose them. They are my sisters. The other pieces of me. Nat is right. I do everything Jack asks me to do. The one thing I will not do, however, is stop seeing my friends.

We carry on dancing and drinking for the rest of the night until the older bouncer comes over to us and tells us they are closing, and we need to leave. As I grab my coat from the cloakroom, Lily trips and falls onto some poor man, who she takes to the floor with her. Me and Nat do nothing to help. We couldn’t help if we wanted to because neither of us are stable on our own feet, but other than the drink, we are both laughing so hard we’re crying. Lily manages to get back up onto her feet and tries apologising to the man who softened her blow but even she is laughing. He scurries away, his face the colour of a tomato.

The laughter soon comes to a stop when we leave the club, and Jack is stood there. Arms crossed with a look that tells me I have messed up big time. You know that look your parents would give you as a kid when you were in trouble?

“Someone is in trouble,” Nat whispers into my ear.

“I haven’t done anything wrong.”

“I know that. So why is he here?”

I shrug at her. Why is he here? I walk over to him with my friends hot on my heels. He can’t shout at me here in front of everyone. There are too many people here who know I have done nothing wrong. I needed this time with my girls. It’s healthy to have a separate life from your significant other.

“Do you really not know how to use your phone?” He snaps at me.

“It’s in my bag. We were dancing, and I didn’t want to drop it.”

“We’re going home right now.” He lunges for me and grabs the top of my arm with such force it will bruise.

“You’re hurting me, Jack. Let me go!” I try to wiggle out of his hold, but he’s dragging me.

“Excuse me, mate, she doesn’t seem to want to go with you,” I hear from behind me. He only said a handful of words to me earlier in the night, but that voice stands out.

Jack stops in his tracks to look at McDreamy; I really should get his name. He towers over him, but it doesn’t put him off. I suppose with his job he’s used to being intimidated by men. He walks over to us and keeps his attention fixed on me. “Do you know this man?” He asks.

“He’s my boyfriend. I’m fine, honestly. Thank you, though,” I say to him. I don’t want to start a fight in the middle of the street surrounded by drunk people. So, I offer him a small smile and hope for the best.

“She hasn’t done anything wrong tonight, pal, so if I were you, I’d let go of her.”

Oh. God. If the ground could swallow me whole right now, I would go willingly. This isn’t happening. It can’t be happening.

"It’s honestly all my fault. Everything is alright. I simply lost track of time and forgot to check in to let him know I was okay." I tell him. I can sense the tears welling up in my eyes, and I know he notices them too, yet he takes a step back. He understands that if he continues to push, it will be me who suffers the consequences, not him.

I nod at him and then offer my friends a smile to say I will be ok, and then I go with him. He practically throws me into the back of a taxi and says nothing until we get home. Once we are out of the taxi, I take a deep breath. I know I have upset him, and he has every right to be angry. I got so lost in my night that I didn’t check in with him when I said I would.

“You won’t be going out with them again,” he says as he grabs my hand to lead me to my front door. “They are bad for you, Olivia.”

“They did nothing wrong. It was me. I was having fun, I didn’t think to check my phone. I’m sorry.”

“So, you were having more fun with them than you do with me?”

“No, Jack. That isn’t what I said. I was letting my hair down and enjoying myself. I was safe. You cannot stop me from seeing my friends.”

He stops and turns to face me, holding my face in his hands. Not like he has done before, but with a force that almost hurts. I’m now officially sober. “You will pick Olivia. It is me, or it is them.”

My brows pull together. “You can’t do that, Jack. That’s not fair. We have been through so much together I won’t turn my back on them.”

“You don’t need them anymore. You have me. Remember what your life was like before me, Liv. You need me.”

Flashbacks of the girl I used to be hit me fast. I don’t want to be that person again. I can’t be that person again. He makes me a better person.

“I’m sorry, ok. I’m so sorry.” The tears I have been holding back flow freely now. “I won’t go out again. Not without you. I am sorry.”

He loosens his hold on my face and rests his forehead on mine. His aftershave costumes my senses, and I feel safe again.

“I love you, Olivia. I just want you to be safe, and you are safe when you are with me.”

“I know I am. I’m sorry.”

“Who was that man?”

I know who he’s talking about, but I really don’t know what to say. In fact, there is nothing to say. It was just a man doing his job. His job is to keep everyone safe.

“The bouncer? He’s good friends with Nat. He hasn’t worked there for very long. I don’t think he lives in town, so he wouldn’t know if we were together or not.”

He pulls away from me. "Why wouldn't you just tell him you are with me?"

"I did."

"No, I mean when you got there. Why didn't you tell him you had a boyfriend."

"I didn't think I needed to? We didn't talk, so I didn't feel the need to say anything. It's a bit weird walking up to a stranger and saying, 'Hi, I have a boyfriend' out of nowhere."

He grabs hold of my hand and drags me the rest of the way. "I saw how he was looking at you, Liv. He thought you were his. You obviously spoke to him, so do not lie to me."

My head is a mess. How was he looking at me? Why was he looking at me? Did I give him the impression I wanted him? Why would he think I am his?

"I'm sure he didn't think that at all, Jack. The only time I spoke to him tonight was when you turned up causing a scene. Do you not trust me at all?"

"It isn't you I don't trust, Liv. It's him."

"He did nothing wrong!" He immediately comes to a stop, "I, I mean, I did nothing wrong."

I follow him into the house and upstairs. When I'm in bed, I try to block out the end of my night and focus on the middle part, the part where I had the best time with my girls. I let Jack do what he wants with me, and I fall asleep.

Chapter 18

Christmas is in two days, and I'm beyond excited.

My nan has been discharged from the hospital and is back in her own bed. She isn't the same, but that's what we expected, if I'm being honest. No one goes through something as big as that and comes out like nothing happened. She is still able to get around with no issues, but it's her eyes that are different. There's a sadness in them. She tells us all she is fine, but it's obvious that she's not. We are so grateful that she is still with us, though.

Rose is due to pop in a few weeks. Her pain is just getting worse by the day, but she powers through. She is prepared now. Everything is washed and put away, and all the furniture that the baby will need has been built. She is going to be the most incredible mum. Growing up, she has always been the most maternal out of the two of us. I always felt awkward around other people's children, but Rose was a natural.

Jack and I have spent a lot of time together. With us both back at work that has meant he has stayed every evening. We are still working through the issues in our relationship. Rome wasn't built in a day, I keep telling myself, but I wish we could be good again. I hate that I upset him, I don't mean to do it, but it seems whatever I do, it isn't good enough for him. I have barely spoken to my friends. When I'm with Jack, he prefers it if I'm not on my phone and I'm giving him my full attention. When I'm at work, I manage to fire Nat and Lily the odd text, but I make sure our conversations are finished before I go home to Jack.

After the night out we had they both messaged me the next day to check everything was ok. I reassured them and told them everything was fine, I just forgot to stay connected with him, and he worried about me. They're both going out tonight, and I would love to go with them, but after last time, I'm not entirely sure it will be worth it. We are finally working things out, and I don't want to mess that up. Both of my friends have voiced their opinions about how Jack shouldn't have grabbed me the way he did. I deleted the messages, though, because I didn't want him to see them and get upset.

We have finished our Christmas shopping, and all of the presents Jack and I got are wrapped and under the tree. He has taken the presents for his family back to his mum and dad's house, so they have them there to open Christmas morning. It's good that he took control this year and told me what to budget for each person. Otherwise, I would have spent way too much money. I always get carried away when buying things for the people I love.

My house is decorated the way it was when we were children, with ceiling decorations, lights in the windows and a big artificial tree. The dog has left it alone this year. Usually, he will try to climb it and ends up pulling it over. All of the decorations are in the traditional Christmas colours: red, green, gold, and silver. My mum has a strong opinion that all decorations should be in that colour scheme, not the pink and navy blue you can buy these days.

I'm lying on my sofa when Jack calls me. He must have just finished work.

"Hey, you," he says to me on the other end of the phone.

"Hey, you just finished?"

"Yeah. Done now for the week, thank God. I was just calling to let you know that I will be going out with Jordan and Dylan tonight."

I didn't think we were going out without each other anymore. I thought that was what he wanted. I use this as my way to tell him that I want to go out with my friends tonight.

"Ok. Lily and Nat are going to go out this evening. I thought I would join them. Is that ok?"

"In town?"

“Yeah, I think they will go to the pub first, then maybe move on to the club after.”

“Well, I’m going out in Colchester, so I won’t be there to look after you.”

Colchester?!

“Why Colchester? I won’t need you to look after me.”

“Because that’s where I want to go. Go if you want to, but do not forget to text me, Olivia.”

We talk a little more about his day and his night out. I told him that I could ask the girls to go out in Colchester if he would be more comfortable with that idea, but he said he would prefer to be with the boys tonight, which is fine because I just want to see my girls again.

After we hang up, I drop a message into our group chat.

Me: Guess who will be joining you tonight?

Nat: SHUT UP?! REALLY?! DO NOT TEASE ME WHITE!!!

Lily: It will be just girls, right?

I roll my eyes at my longest friend's message. Lily was the most shaken up by what happened that night. He didn’t do anything I didn’t deserve. He would never hurt me in the ways she seems to think he’s capable of.

Me: Yes Lil. Just girls.

Me: I do have work tomorrow, but I’m not due until lunchtime.

Lily: Where is Jack?

Me: Colchester.

Nat: Why?

Me: He said that’s where he wanted to go. What are we wearing?

Nat: He wants to go an hour away from you after telling you he wanted to spend more time with you? Bit weird that, mate.

We spend the next hour sharing outfit ideas and deciding on where we will go. We decided both the girls would come here after they are ready so we can have a drink before venturing into town. We also decided that jeans were a must because of how cold it is now, only if you have glitter on you somewhere. I own no glittery tops, so I am hoping glitter on my eyes and cheeks will be enough to please them.

Once I am ready, I fire Jack a quick photo on Snapchat to get his approval. I don't want people to get the wrong idea. I don't think my outfit is too revealing, but you never know.

My hair is braided and fastened to the back of my head with hundreds of bobby pins, like an upside-down plait crown. I have left my face framing out and curled it loosely, so it hangs the way I like it. Jack loves my hair like this, so I know that it's ok. My makeup is slightly different tonight. I have still applied the layers of foundation, contour, and blusher, but I have added a touch of highlighter to accentuate my already sharp cheekbones. I got it from MUA, and it is so incredibly pigmented. I have managed to pull off an amazing Smokey eye look and used Drip Drip by Made by Mitchell on the inner half of my lids to brighten the look up and, of course, add the glitter I need. I have applied a set of false lashes and a red lip. As it is Christmas I believe you must go all out.

The outfit is quite simple: a high-waisted pair of black skinny jeans, a staple every girl should have in their wardrobe, paired with a white corset top. Now, I know that does, in fact, sound revealing, but with my black oversized blazer on top, it covers what needs to be covered, my cleavage and the fading bruise on my arm from where Jack grabbed me.

Jack hasn't opened the Snapchat I sent him yet, so I send him a text message telling him to check it. For the first time in what feels like forever, I look at myself in the mirror, and I love the girl staring back at me. She looks put together and happy. I don't have to force myself to smile tonight because I'm excited to spend this time with my friends. I chuck my phone into my black clutch bag and make my way downstairs to the kitchen.

“Wow,” my mum stops scrolling on her phone when she sees me, “you look incredible.”

This wins her a smile. “Thank you. I feel incredible.”

“You will get too hot in that blazer, though. You know that, right?”

“Well, I’m not naked underneath, so I am sure if I get too hot, I can take it off. You know what it’s like, though, they’ll probably still have the air conditioning on in the middle of December.”

“Where’s Jack tonight?”

What is everyone’s obsession with having to know where this man is tonight? Am I not allowed out on my own?

I tell my mum about him being with his brother tonight and the fact that he isn’t in town. She tells me it’s good to have time away from each other. It isn’t healthy to live in each other's pockets all of the time. I can see where she’s coming from, but I still feel anxious about him being so far away from me if I do indeed need his help. After spending so much of my free time with him, I feel lost without him by my side.

I pour my friends, and I each an extraordinarily strong glass of pink gin and lemonade and a shot of some cherry liquor, which I’m sure has been in the back of our cupboard for longer than I have been alive.

Lily arrives first, she is wearing the same outfit she wore the last time we went out, but this time has paired it with a silver sequin bag and matching strappy heels. She has curled the ends of her hair and has even added a faint shimmery eyeshadow to her lids.

“Oh, shotgun on borrowing that top first,” my friend says as a way of greeting.

I hand her both of the drinks I poured for her and give her my best courtesy. “You don’t think it’s too revealing?” I ask

“No, why? Who said that?”

“No one. I just don’t want to get hit on tonight.”

“Olivia, have you seen yourself? Even blind men would be able to sense how pretty you are.” She necks her shot and puts a hand on her hip.

"This isn't Jack, is it? Do *not* let him make you feel like you cannot wear what you want. You have worn far more revealing outfits than this in the past."

I let out a long breath and take my shot before adding, "No, it isn't him. I just don't want to give people the wrong idea. He got upset about McDreamy eyeing me up last time."

"The man was doing his job, Liv."

"I told him that, but he said it was more than that."

Lily opens her mouth to respond as Nat comes barging through the door. "It's Baltic out there."

"Well, then, we best get an alcohol blanket on before we leave," I say to her.

"Nat. What do you think of Liv's outfit?" Lily cocks her head.

"Lil. Just leave it."

"No. You can't let a man tell you how you should and shouldn't be dressing. Nat?"

"I thought we were in for a fun night." Nat rolls her eyes. "You look fine, Liv. Does it matter if he doesn't like it?"

"Yes." I rest my hands on top of my head. "Yes, it does."

"The day a man tells me what to wear, please kill me." Lily rolls her eyes before pouring herself another shot. "The boy told her the bouncer was eyeing her up when he was just doing his job."

Nat turns her head to look at me. "Liv?"

"Just drop it. Please. Can we just have fun tonight?"

We spend the next hour playing Ring of Fire, which I can tell you is not a game for the weak. By the time we leave the house, none of us can see straight, we all have the giggles, and Natalia has already broken a nail. Nat's outfit is similar to mine. The only difference is she has a black sequin corset top on instead. Her hair is curled and pulled back into a half-up and half-down hairstyle. She is so effortlessly beautiful all the time it kind of gets annoying.

The pub is already busy by the time we get there, we have a quick scan and realise there's no table to sit at. None of us feel like standing when there isn't any music to dance to. Nat tells us the club will already be open. It will be empty, but that never bothers us. We decide that an empty nightclub is far more fun than an overpacked pub. At least there will be music, and as it's still early, the DJ will likely play whatever we ask him to, well, whatever Natalia asks him to play.

"Lewis! My favourite bouncer," Natalia shouts to the bouncer at the door.

So, McDreamy does, in fact, have a name. A name that suits him. Most Lewis's I've met have all had blonde hair and blue eyes. I usually stay away from them as well because they tend to be bad news.

"There was me thinking tonight would be an easy one. You just had to be out with your entourage tonight, didn't you," he turns to her with the biggest smile on his face.

"Remember I am the one paying your wages tonight, Mr," she says whilst poking a finger into his chest.

"Judging at the sight of you. I would say you have already had enough."

Natalia blows a raspberry at him, like the mature woman she is and pushes past him. Me and Lily follow closely behind. I try to avoid eye contact with him, but he puts his arm out in front of me to stop me from passing. I look up to try and reach for Lily, but she is too far ahead to save me.

"Are you ok?" Lewis asks me. His blue eyes searching mine for an answer.

"I'm fine. He isn't here tonight, so don't worry, I won't need your services." Why does drunk me have to be an arsehole to every man that tries talking to me? Also, services? What is he? An escort or something? Jesus Christ.

“I was only trying to help. I’m sorry, I just don’t believe it’s ok for a man to hurt a woman.”

“For your information, the bruise is almost gone.” I chuckle humourlessly at myself. Drunk me is also too honest.

“He left a bruise?” His voice is deep and raspy.

I let out a big sigh and roll my eyes at him. “It isn’t like I didn’t deserve it. Now let me through.”

The horror on this man’s face right now. I don’t expect anyone to understand, he didn’t hurt me because he was angry at me. He was just worried about me, and it was my fault he was worrying. Lewis lowers his arm and gives me a nod as I pass him. Hopefully, I will be able to avoid him for the rest of the night. One awkward interaction is enough for me.

I find my friends on the dance floor with a drink in their hands. I hung my blazer up at the cloakroom, it isn’t as cold in here as I thought it would be. When the club starts to fill up, I can always go and collect it and cover myself up.

“Where the hell were you?” Lily asks, eying my arm.

I nod to the bar, and she follows me over, “Lewis wanted to see if I was ok after what happened with Jack.”

“That’s nice of him.”

“No Lil, it isn’t. I don’t need people worrying about me and my relationship. It’s my fault he got angry, no one else’s. Can we just drop it?”

She gives me a nod, but I don’t believe for one second she is ok with the conversation being dropped. She worries about me more than most people do, but I would tell her if I thought I was in any real danger.

“Lil I’m ok. Nothing bad is going to happen to me. I can look after myself. It was my fault ok. Mine.”

“I just… Ok.”

It’s not long before the club quickly fills up with people, Natalia gestures for us to go outside for a minute to cool down. We weave through the sea of people and make our way into the smoking area. I can tell it's cold, because of the people coming into the club with their scarves and coats on, but I can't feel it, I've had too much to drink. I pull my phone out of my bag and check to see if I have heard anything from Jack, I haven't. I leave it on the table whilst we are out here, so if it goes off, I'll see it.

"Merry Christmas bitches!" Natalia shouts with her glass raised.

"Another Christmas pretending Santa isn't creepy as fuck!" I raise my glass to her.

We turn to Lily "Another Christmas alone and single," she says way too sadly, but she raises her glass as well.

"You will find someone Lily. There are over seven billion people on this earth, it will just take time to find the one person that's right for you." I rest my head on her shoulder.

"I know. But I just seem to meet horrible boys. The nice ones don't want me."

"Enough of that!" Nat swipes at her from across the table. "Be happy on your own! There is nothing more attractive than a woman that knows what she wants!"

"I love you both. Can we just get married to each other?" Lily asks pouting at us.

"If we are all single by thirty, I say we do it." I raise my glass and the others follow suit.

The downstairs DJ starts playing Numb by Linkin Park, we all glance at each other and then race for the door. How none of us stack it I will never know. I'm not sure when Daisy and Georgia got here but they're already screaming to the song when we walk in. I lead my friends over to them and in a circle we all sing and dance with each other for the next three minutes. Just girls having fun.

When the next song starts to play, I turn from my friends to the direction of the bar to get us all a shot. As I'm on my way over, I notice that Lewis is stood at the door watching me, he nods his head in the direction of the exit and disappears. For a minute I debate ignoring him, but something in my gut tells me to follow him out.

He's talking to the club owner when I make it outside, asking for a five-minute break as he needs to take care of something. It’s then I click my phone in his hand, and my heart falls out of my mouth. I must have left it on the table when we rushed back inside. The owner nods at him and takes up the spot at the main door as Lewis grabs my hand and leads me back inside silently. We pass my friends on the dance floor, and I widen my eyes at them with a *help* look on my face, but it’s no use, they can’t see me through the crowd. He leads me to a tiny staff room and closes the door behind us.

The room is full of different types of alcohol, with a small worn wooden table and a single chair. There are stacks of paperwork on the table, none of it seems to be organised. I wouldn’t be able to function in such an environment, but then again, I don’t know what it’s like to run a club.

“You left this on the table,” he waves my phone at me, “you let him talk to you this way?”

“Who?”

“You know who.”

“I don’t remember giving you permission to go through my phone.” I reach for it, but he snatches it back.

“I didn’t go through it. I was hoping the wallpaper would give me an indication of who the phone belonged to. It isn’t my fault his message popped up.”

“I’m sorry, but it isn’t really any of your business,” I say, trying to keep my voice level.

“People can help you, you know? You can get out of this.”

“I really don’t know what you’re talking about. There is nothing to get out of.”

“Really?” He gently brushes his fingers over the bruise on my arm.

"I told you. I deserved it."

My phone buzzes again in his hand, and he breaks eye contact with me to check the notification. "Un-fucking-believable." He shakes his head.

"What?" I ask

"Look yourself. You might want to rethink who you spend your time with." He hands me my phone and leaves me in the room alone.

With a shaky hand, I look down at my phone.

Jack: I can't believe you actually went out. After all the things that we spoke about. You filthy little whore. You are so desperate for attention.

Jack: Now I hear you are in a private room alone with that bouncer? You fucking slut.

I feel sick. He said it was ok for me to go out tonight. He has done the same thing. How does he know Lewis took me to one side? I close my eyes, and the tears start falling. I drop to the floor and hold my head in my hands. I need to get out of here.

Me: You said I could go? He was giving me my phone back I left it outside.

Jack: It was a test, Olivia, and you failed. I hope you're happy with yourself. He will never care for you the way I do.

Me: I don't want him to care for me. I don't want anyone else, Jack. I want you.

Jack: You make me sick.

I can't breathe. I feel like someone is smothering me. I have to get out of here. I pull up the Snapchat app on my phone to assess the damage. There's no saving my makeup. It's a mess. Mascara is running down my face. My friends can't see me this way. Not after I insisted earlier that they let it go, I assured them everything was fine. If they catch me crying, they will never be ok with me being with him ever again.

There is a back set of steps that lead from the downstairs area to upstairs. I will have to slip out of this room and up the stairs that are immediately to my left. That's the only way my friends won't see me. With a deep breath, I open the door and make my way up the stairs. Time slows down when I open the door to the top dance floor. The lights are flashing, and slowly, everyone starts to look at me. I put my head down and push past everyone to the front set of stairs. My breathing is uneven, and my vision is blurred.

Somehow, I manage it. I hand my ticket over to the man in the cloakroom. It's just my luck it's someone I used to go to school with. He takes one look at me, and as his mouth opens to say something, he obviously sees something in my eyes and decides against it. I wouldn't even know what to say to him if he did ask if I was ok. He hands my blazer over to me, and as I turn to walk away, I hear him on the radio, alerting every member of staff in this place that I am having some kind of mental breakdown. *Great.*

I put my blazer on and head for the door. I make it halfway up the hill from the club when everything I was holding in comes bursting out. I have experienced many panic attacks before, but this one feels entirely different. My mind is racing, a jumbled mess of anxious thoughts. I can't focus, can't catch my breath, can barely see straight. I slide down the nearest wall, and cradle my head in my hands, desperately trying to recall the coping techniques from all those anxiety workshops I have attended. Slowly, I begin to focus on my breathing, forcing myself to take deep, steady inhales and exhales.

After five minutes my breathing is more even, and I decide to stand. Only then do I see Lewis making his way up the hill. I shake my head at him and turn to walk away, but he reaches me before I manage to run off.

"Are you ok? We've been looking for you. What happened?" He asks.

"Do I look ok to you?" I shout in his face, " you know what happened. Is this what you wanted?"

"I was only trying to help Jesus Christ." He reaches for my arm, but I shake him off.

"I don't need your help. You don't even know me! You have no idea what you have done." A sob breaks free. "You have ruined everything."

"I ruined everything. By giving you your phone back? By telling you that you can get out of this?"

"By even looking in my direction. If you just stayed away. If you just didn't speak to me. He wouldn't be this mad at me. He would still want me. You. Ruined. Everything."

I look him dead in the eye as I say the last bit. I shake my head at him and turn away to start my walk home.

Chapter 19

Christmas has always been a challenging time for my family. We try to enjoy it, but it has been hard since my grandad passed away. He died a few days after Christmas, and since then, it has just been a reminder that he's not here. I still have the last thing he ever bought me. It's a Furby, pink and white. My sister got one for Christmas, and I fell in love with hers, so he got me my own. It still works, but I have taken the batteries out; otherwise, it just talks to itself in the middle of the night and scares the life out of me. I have started to think she may actually be haunted. It's something I will keep until I pass away. My last reminder of him.

We have never woken up early for Christmas. Rose and I would sleep in until eight, which is apparently not normal no matter what your age. However, this morning is different. Rose comes bursting through my bedroom door before seven and tells me to get up. She leaves and does the same to my parents. Before I get up, I rub my eyes and exhale deeply. I haven't seen Jack since our argument. We have messaged each other a few times. He hasn't said sorry for the things he said, but I have apologised numerous times for going out when I shouldn't have.

I take my phone off charge and check my notifications, which are full of messages from my friends.

Nat: Merry Christmas Bitches!

Lily: You too!

Instantly, I feel a wave of shame. My friends tried to contact me that night, wondering where I had gone. I ignored their messages until the following evening. I apologised for disappearing, but I didn't tell them the real reason. I just told them that I was sick, and Lewis told me I needed to go home. While it doesn't guarantee he won't mention anything to

Natalia during their next shift together, for the moment, I have postponed the inevitable.

Me: Merry Christmas, angel girls! Have a drink for me. Love you xx

Then I notice I've been added to another group chat with Georgia, Daisy, Jordan, Dylan, and Jack. Georgia is the one who set it up. As irresponsible as she can be sometimes, she does everything in her power to keep us all together.

Georgia: Merry Xmas!

Jordan: Do we really need a group chat for that?

Dylan: Read my mind, mate

Georgia: Don't be such a Grinch!

Daisy: Merry Christmas, grumpy boys!

Me: I love a group chat G, don't worry! Merry Christmas x

Georgia: THANK YOU!

Jack has messaged me separately. Granted, it isn't a long message, but it's still a message.

Jack: Happy Christmas.

At least he thought about me this morning. I know it's going to take him a while to forgive me for being so reckless. So, I choose to ignore the bluntness and just feel grateful that he sent the message in the first place.

Me: Merry Christmas. I love you x

My sister is back by the time I've caught up with my messages. I chuckle at the sight of her in her Christmas PJs. My mum gets us matching each year. Some families choose to dress up on Christmas day, but our family tradition is to get out of one set of PJs and put on another. This year's set is a replica of Santa's outfit. They look even funnier on her, with her growing baby belly acting as Santa's real belly. I'm sure my mum didn't do it on purpose, but it's still funny either way.

"Get out of bed. I've been up for hours." Rose drags the covers from me.

I groan at her, "I. Am. Coming. Not all of us are morning people like you."

She puts a hand on her hip and cocks her head. "You have five minutes to get downstairs, or I will burn all of your Christmas presents."

"You wouldn't."

She raises a brow at me with a '*want-to-bet*' look on her face. I choose not to challenge her. I have doubted her before, and it has backfired in my face. She's heavily pregnant now as well, so I know it's not worth the risk with her unpredictable hormones.

"Ok. I'm coming." I say to her, as I get out of my bed. I find the PJs my mum got us and go to the bathroom to change before heading downstairs to start the day with my family.

Every year, we follow the same routine. My mum and Rose prepare tea and coffee for everyone, while I begin to sift through the gifts beneath the tree, organising them into piles for where each person will be sitting. Rob and my dad lounge on the sofa, grumbling about being awake at such an early hour. By the time I've finished distributing the presents, we all have a drink loaded with caffeine and sugar.

We open them the same way every year as well, Rose and I will open ours whilst our parents sit and watch us. Our dad is as surprised as we are as we open our presents. He puts money towards them, but he lets our mum take control of what's bought. I do think sometimes that's because he wouldn't have a clue when it comes to shopping for us. Unless we wanted a football kit. Next, Rob opens his, followed by our mum and dad.

I say this every year, but my mother has truly excelled. This year, she has managed to get me everything I subtly suggested I'd like over the past few months. Makeup, clothing, gift vouchers, and naturally, the usual hair ties, facial cleanser, shower gel, and cozy socks. She always purchases items for us that we wouldn't typically buy for ourselves, the kinds of things that often get overlooked.

When we're all finished, my dad goes into the kitchen to start preparing our fry-up breakfast, another tradition I will continue to do, no matter what my age. My dad doesn't cook often, but when he does, it's always incredible. I take this time to thank Mum for everything she got me. I'm not sure how much Christmas will change when Rose and I each have our own families, so I want to soak this one up.

I sit back for a minute and just take my family in. My mum fought tirelessly for us to have the best life possible, and I know there are times she doubts whether she has done a good enough job at it, but in my eyes, she's done everything perfectly. This woman went through hell and back and still managed to get through it all whilst raising two children. She inspires me to be the best version of myself. I want her to be proud of me every single day for the rest of her life. I never want her to feel let down by me. She has done so much for us that I owe her this. I owe everything to her.

We all eat breakfast and spend the rest of the morning calling different family members on Facetime. My nan is spending Christmas with my uncle this year. It is strange that she isn't here with us, but I am so happy she isn't alone.

My mum always makes the most incredible Christmas dinner. I will uphold that belief for the entirety of my life. Every Wednesday, she serves a fantastic roast dinner, but her Christmas one is simply unmatched. We have a variety of meats to choose from, including turkey, beef, and gammon. The roast potatoes are prepared in goose fat; this is the only occasion during the year when she uses it. They turn out crispy and golden on the outside while being fluffy like clouds on the inside. Alongside it, we enjoy the traditional Yorkshire puddings, stuffing, and heaps of vegetables to accompany the meal.

We are sat here now with full stomachs, paper crowns on our heads from pulling crackers, and half-empty glasses of wine.

"That was incredible, Mum, thank you," I say to her across the table.

"She's been preparing for it mentally all week." Dad adds

"You try cooking for this many people without having a plan." My mum glares at him.

"Why would I? When I have you to do it for me." He raises his glass to his mouth to try to hide the smile there.

"Well, next year, you can do it yourself," she replies, getting up from the table to start taking the dirty dishes to the dishwasher. My dad chuckles silently, knowing his blow hit exactly the way he intended it to.

"Looks like we'll all be having beans on toast then."

"You do that then. I'll book myself a nice trip away on a tropical island away from you all!"

I can never get enough of watching their dynamic. Their witty banter and playful teasing. It's so obvious to everyone around them that they love each other so deeply. Their relationship is what I aspire to have one day. An unconditional love that will withstand the test of time. I do believe I can have that with Jack one day.

Chapter 20

I must fall asleep on the sofa after dinner. Christmas day is not complete without an after-dinner nap, in my opinion. Jack is the one who wakes me.

“Hey, sleepyhead, time to wake up,” he whispers into my ear, tucking my hair behind it.

I groan as I open my eyes. I am still too full to be awake right now. He smiles down at me, his eyes fixed on mine. Those eyes that I fell in love with all those months ago. Every time he looks at me, I am consumed by them. My heart skips a beat, and my breath is taken away. I give him a smile of my own.

“Come upstairs. I have something for you,” he says as he takes my hands to help me up. The rest of my family are spread across the sofa asleep. My mum's dinner has defeated us all.

As Jack guides me up to my bedroom, I can't help but gasp when he opens the door. I have no clue what time he arrived, but my bed is filled with rose petals. On either side of a small box, two large bouquets are placed.

“What is this?” I ask him with my hands on my chest.

“Open it and see.” He pushes against my lower back to usher me into the room.

I’m trembling right now. All I want is to share my life with Jack, yet deep down, I really secretly wish that there isn't an engagement ring in that box. We have so many issues to resolve before we can take on such a significant commitment. It says something about my ego that I am even considering the possibility of an engagement ring being inside.

I grab the box and take a seat on the edge of my bed. As I glance up at him, I notice he's biting his bottom lip. *Is he feeling anxious?* When I lift the lid of the cream box, I discover a ring nestled inside. Time seems to stop. I hold my breath. The ring is a delicate silver band featuring two interlinked hearts. I look back at him, a frown forming on my forehead.

"It's a promise ring," he says, walking over to me to join me on my bed.

"What for?" I can't say I've ever heard of a promise ring before.

"Think of it as a pre-engagement ring. It's me promising that I want to spend my life with you, Olivia. It represents my love for you, me being faithful to you. It means that one day, I want to marry you."

Tears blur my vision. "You want to marry me?"

"I do," he chuckles. "Not right now, but in the future, yes. This ring proves how serious I am about our relationship." He takes the box from my hand and takes the ring out. "So, what do you say, Miss White?"

A million different thoughts are running through my mind, but before I let them consume me, I nod at him. When he slides the ring on my finger, the tears I have been holding back start to flow freely.

"I love you, Olivia." He wipes the tears from my face.

"I love you too." I finally make eye contact with him. This is it, everything I have ever wished for. This man right in front of me is my happily ever after. "I thought you hated me."

"Oh, baby, I could never hate you."

For the next hour, we lay on my bed, wrapped in each other's arms, discussing our future and reminiscing about our Christmas mornings. Jack spent his with his family, one of his nans came over and joined them for the dinner his mum made. He mentioned they spent the day watching movies together. Reflecting on it, I realise our Christmas celebrations aren't all that different. We both enjoy the day surrounded by family, relaxing on the sofa, and indulging in plenty of food. This gives me hope that when we start our own family, it won't be too different from how we spend our days now.

As we hear sounds of movement from downstairs, we find a way to separate from each other. Jack mentioned that he had a conversation with my parents regarding the promise ring before buying it. They were thrilled with the concept and expressed that they already considered him a member of the family. The knowledge that they are pleased for me gives me an extra bounce in my step as we head down to join them.

"Where did you go?" Rose asks me with her hands on her hips, ready to bite my head off.

I show her the ring on my finger, excited to see her reaction, but it isn't the reaction I was after. She snatches my hand and frowns at the small ring on my finger. When she looks up at me, she swallows hard, and her brows draw together. "You got engaged?"

"No," I say as I snatch my hand from her. "It's a promise ring."

"Never heard of it," she says, raising her brows now. "Don't you think it's all a bit quick?"

"It isn't what you think," Jack says from behind me. "It's just a ring that promises I'm faithful to her."

"You need a ring to promise my sister that?"

Oh dear.

"No. But it is pretty. It isn't like I'm ever going to marry her."

My jaw hits the floor. I turn my head slowly to look at him. My eyes are practically bulging out of my skull. "What?" I say.

"It's just a ring, Olivia. It symbolises me being faithful and only wanting you."

"That isn't what you said upstairs." My brows pull together, and I fiddle with the ring on my finger.

We have an audience now. Dad has paused the TV, and I am aware that all eyes are on us.

"Yes, it is!" His voice is getting louder and louder by the second, "I said it shows you I am faithful to you. Do not make this out to be something it isn't. Why would I want to marry you after everything you have done!"

I open my mouth to speak, but nothing comes out. I turn to my family sitting on the sofa and they're all looking at me like I have lost my mind. I chance a look at Rose beside me. She is fixated on Jack. The look in her eye tells me she is thinking of all the ways she could kill him.

Rose was always there to defend me growing up. One time, when we were at the same middle school, a boy in her year group came up to me at lunchtime and shouted in my face. I found Rose and cried to her about it. I was only in year five at the time, and they were in year eight. Later, when she got home, I heard her talking to our mum about it. He was riding his bike home, and he rode up to her and was laughing about how he made me cry. Rose saw red and punched him in the side of the head, knocking him off his bike in front of all of his friends. He stayed away from me after that. The look in her eye right now is the same one that I saw that day when I went to her.

Jack grabs my arm to turn me back towards him. "I got you the ring to prove to you that *I* am faithful. I got it before *you* disappeared with that bouncer the other night. Why don't you tell your family how unfaithful you actually are, Olivia."

"That isn't what happened, Jack. We have been through this. Let go of me. You're hurting me."

He looks past me to my parents as he says, "I had to hear about it from one of my friends. She didn't even have the decency to tell me." He looks me in the eye, then as he drops my arm, "I am going home, to the people that really appreciate me."

With that, he storms to the front door and slams it shut behind him. I collapse on the floor, my body trembling from the sobs escaping me. I thought we were ok. I thought we were moving past this. I know I still have some making up to do. He told me he wanted to marry me, *didn't he?* Did I just make it up again?

The panic sets in, my mind filling with a number of voices and racing thoughts. My vision tunnels, darkening around the edges, as my breathing becomes erratic and uneven. A crushing tightness constricts my chest, the pain spreading like a vice. I rub at it frantically, desperate to ease the discomfort, to draw in a full breath, but nothing seems to work. The panic attack has me firmly in its grip.

I feel a hand on my shoulder. From the gentleness of the touch, I know it's my mum. "I. Can't. Breathe."

"Yes, you can, baby," she says, shushing me. "Count with me, ok?"

My mum leads me through a breathing exercise, inhale for five seconds, hold it for four, then exhale for another five, until my breathing steadies and the pain in my chest subsides. She holds me on the floor until I'm ready to move. This isn't the first time she has had to do this, and I can guarantee it will not be the last. I'm so broken. Nothing can fix me, this is just who I am now.

"Go upstairs and run yourself a bath." She kisses the crown of my head.

I look up at her, then, "I didn't do it, Mum. I didn't do what he said I did. My…My head is a mess."

"I know you wouldn't, baby. That's not who you are. There will always be people out there who are jealous of your relationship. Some people are so miserable in their own lives that they will try to sabotage other people's happiness."

"That son of a bitch." My sister shouts as she lunges for the front door. She's fast, but my mum is faster, grabbing her hand to hold her back. "Let. Me Go."

"What are you going to do, Rose? Think it through." My mum eyes my sister's belly.

It's then I see the tears streaming down her face. She knows I struggle with my mental health, but I keep much of it hidden from her. I don't want her to worry about me, when she has finally got everything she has ever wanted in life. I hate burdening other people with how I'm feeling. Usually, I keep it hidden from my mum as well. I don't want her to think she has failed. My head is like this because of my own life, not the life she has given me, but the one I have tried to build for myself.

"What the hell happened?" Rose asks me.

I let out a big sigh. "I left my phone on the table in the smoking area the other night. The bouncer found it."

"And?" My sister says as she crosses her arms on top of her growing bump.

My mind is so foggy, I feel so confused about what has and has not actually happened, but I tell my family what I believe happened the other night. "And he found me on the dance floor. I was with Georgia, Daisy, Lily, and Natalia. He nodded towards the staff room, and I followed him. He then showed me he had my phone, and when I went to take it back, he wouldn't let me have it."

"Why?" My mum asks me, frowning.

"Because. Ugh, when he picked it up, he looked at the wallpaper to see who it belonged to, and he saw a text message. A not very nice message, and he asked me about it. He ended up giving it back in the end and I walked home."

"Who was it from?" Rob is stood next to Rose now.

Rob has also saved me from danger more than one time. The one that stands out is the night I got spiked when I was eighteen. He found me at the bar with a guy he knew I had been avoiding for most of my teenage life. He was holding my unconscious body up against the bar. Rob and Rose had only been dating for a brief time, but he still helped me. He told the man he would get me home safe, they argued a little bit, but then Jordan caught wind of it and backed Rob up. Together, they carried me from the club and took me home to my mum, who took me to the hospital. It wasn't until I met Georgia that night, that I realised Jordan had been looking out for me this whole time.

They confirmed what we already knew. I still don't remember anything from that night at all. Rob told me he saw me kissing him before things went south. After the kiss he kept watching us to make sure I was consenting to it all. When it was obvious that I couldn't give consent for anything, that's when he intervened. I dread to think what could have happened that night if he didn't help me. I still see him from time to time around town, and every time, I feel physically sick to my stomach.

"It was from Jack."

"And what did he say that was bad enough for a stranger to question you?" Rose asks.

"Rose!" My mum warns her.

"It's fine, Mum. He said he was disappointed in me for going out. I told him I wouldn't go out anymore as it makes him worry when I do. That's when someone told him I disappeared with the bouncer. He then texted me again and called me a slut."

I look at the shock on their faces. Why are they shocked? I did this to myself. If I had listened to him, then I wouldn't be in this situation right now. I chose to go out that night. I knew it would upset him, even though he said it was ok.

"Go for a bath, Olivia." My mum says as she walks back into the front room with her hands balled into fists.

I go to protest, but Rose gives me a look that says, '*Just drop it and do as she says.*' So, I turn and walk up the stairs and run myself a bath.

Chapter 21

Harriet

"Well?" My oldest daughter says behind me.

"Rose, please."

I have noticed the differences in my youngest daughter recently. I haven't said anything to her because I know when she is ready to talk about it, she will. She has always been an open book with me. She has been more secretive, and I know she thinks she has been hiding it well, but I am her mother. I know her better than anyone else on this planet. I raised her. She has been more withdrawn as well. I know it's normal for children to spend less time with their parents as they get older, but she has stopped seeing her friends as much, too.

Lily and Natalia have practically lived here since the day they became friends. Lately, though, I've hardly seen them. I thought perhaps they had fallen out, but now I know that Jack is behind this, I wonder how deep this controlling behaviour runs. Is it him that's stopped her from seeing them?

I didn't want this for my girls. They have been through enough. They deserve to find someone who loves them for the strong, independent women I raised them to be.

"Do you have Lily's number?" I ask Rose as I sit on the sofa next to my husband.

"I think so. I got it for when we were planning Liv's surprise party. That was a few years ago, though. She could have changed her number by now." My heavily pregnant daughter lowers herself onto the sofa next to her boyfriend.

She reads the number off to me, and I send Lily a message.

Me: Hi Lily, It's Harriet, Olivia's mum. Is this still your number?

"What are you going to do?" Rose asks, rubbing her growing bump.

"I'm going to speak to Lily. She knows Olivia as well as we all do. I am hoping she has confided in her, or perhaps she has at least seen something from when they have all been together."

"You could just ask Liv," Lee says from beside me.

My husband is amazing with my girls. Him and Olivia are so alike that when people see them together, they would never know that they are not blood-related. He really jumped in the deep end when we got together. I always thought my family was complete, just me and my girls, but the day I met Lee I knew we'd secretly been missing something.

I put my hand on his thigh and let out a big sigh. "I could. I know that. I have been through this, though, Lee. The chances of her being honest with me right now are slim."

My phone buzzes, and we all hold our breath.

Lily: Hi Harriet. This is still my number, yes. Is everything ok? Merry Christmas to you and Lee!

Tears fill my eyes; I feel so relieved.

Me: Merry Christmas to you, too, sweetheart. I need to talk to you about Olivia. She is ok but we are worried about her. She is at work tomorrow. Would you be able to pop over? I know it's Christmas, but I wouldn't ask unless it was serious.

Lily: Of course. What time does she leave?

Me: She will be there by eight. Anytime between then and when she finishes will be ok.

Lily: I can come around ten.

Me: Thank you, Lily. I will see you then. Please don't say anything to her.

I fill my family in on the plan. I have asked that they are not here when Lily is. Lily is a shy girl, like Olivia. They are practically the same person. The audience may make her nervous, and she may not be completely honest with me.

Our Christmas evening is different to previous ones, as well as my mum not being here, we all try to make Olivia forget about the earlier altercation, but I can see the sadness in her eyes. I wish I could make it all go away. I wish I could hold her like I did as a child and sing her worries away, but I can't.

The next morning, I stay in bed until I hear Olivia leave for work. Then I get up and get myself dressed for the day. The best outcome today is Lily telling me there is nothing more than what Olivia has mentioned. Her telling me that the thoughts that kept me awake all night were just that, thoughts. My biggest fear is my girls going through what I did with Richard. We don't talk about it. I would if they wanted to, but I never bring him up unless they do first. I know Olivia struggles with the memories of him more than Rose does. I was hoping those memories would keep her away from men like him.

Lily knocks on the door twice before she lets herself in. As I said before, she used to basically live here so I told her many years ago to just let herself in.

"Hey," she calls out.

"Hi love, I'm in the kitchen," I shout back to her.

She comes in and gives me a tight hug before sitting in the chair next to me. She lets out a big sigh and offers me a small smile.

"I am so sorry to ask you to do this. I just know that if I ask her for the truth, she won't give it to me," I say

"It's fine. I have been worried about her, too. She tells me everything is ok, but I know it isn't." Tears line her eyes as she continues, "I feel like I've let her down, but I know she won't listen to me."

I reach a hand out across the table to hold hers. “Why don’t I just tell you what I know, and then you can tell me what you know?”

She nods at me, so I tell her about yesterday's altercation. I tell her about the promise ring that we had no idea about, how he called her out in front of her entire family before storming out, and then how Olivia told us about the message she received from him.

“Your turn.” I squeeze her hand.

“Ok. Well, she hasn’t spoken to me or Nat much since that night out. She just disappeared. She didn’t tell us she was leaving, and she didn’t tell us the real reason. She said she was sick, and the bouncer sent her home. We certainly had no idea about the ring. Things were good at the beginning, she was so happy, and he really did try to make her a better person. He loved her in a way that I was jealous of, a way that I dream of being loved one day. I can’t tell you when things went south. I know he took her for a few nights away. She told us on our girl's night that they had a lot of talks about their relationship and what is and isn’t working.”

She looks down at the table. “That’s when I saw how terrible things were. We had the best time dancing and singing with each other, so much so that she forgot to check her phone. When we were kicked out at the end of the night he was stood outside. She froze instantly, and her entire mood changed. She walked over to him, and when we got closer, I could see how mad he was. He grabbed her so hard he hurt her. She told him he was hurting her, but he just squeezed her arm harder. The bouncer tried intervening then, but Jack stood his ground. Olivia told him it was nothing to worry about, and he backed away. I don’t know what happened after that. We asked her if she was ok, and she said she was. When we went out the night she disappeared, and she took the blazer off, I could see what was left of the bruise on her arm.” She wipes the tears from her face. “I am so sorry, Harriet. I have let her down.”

I pull my hand from hers, then. *My poor baby.* I wipe my own tears away, and we sit in silence for a few minutes.

“Please don’t think you’ve let her down, Lily. You did the right thing by telling me. At least now we can come up with a plan to help her.”

"You need to get her away from him, Harriet. Please."

"It isn't always that simple, Lily. If we tell her to leave him, we risk pushing her away from us."

"There has to be something we can do."

"We wait. We protect her the best we can until then, but we have to wait. She has to realise it for herself."

We spend the next hour together catching up about life. I try to reassure her again when she leaves that she has done the right thing. When she has gone, I add Lee and Rose into a chat titled "Baby" just in case Olivia checks my phone.

Me: I spoke to Lily. It isn't good.

Rose: What do you mean?

Me: I'm not going to give you all the details. I just need you to be there for Liv.

Lee: I will do whatever you need me to do, but I will not have him back in our house.

Me: We risk pushing her away if we do that.

Rose: He is not coming anywhere near me or my baby.

Me: Rose, this is not about you or the baby. This is about Olivia.

Chapter 22

When I come back from work, I notice my mum sitting on the couch with a book in her hands. She seems to have tears in her eyes, and knowing she reads thrillers, it certainly isn't because of that.

"Are you ok?" I ask as I take my shoes and coat off before joining her on the sofa.

"I'm fine, baby," she looks up from her book and offers me a small smile. "Have you heard from Jack?"

"Not yet. I am going to ask him if we can talk, though."

"That's good. Maybe you can talk to him somewhere else, away from here, like neutral ground."

"Ok. I'll have a shower, and then I will give him a text." I kiss the top of her head and get up.

I know she's hiding something from me. I am so much like my mum that I know all of the signs. The shower is a welcome friend after the day I've had, though, so I leave her sat there. She will talk to me when she is ready to, I'm sure of it.

The Boxing Day sales were in full swing today. I arrived at work early to put stickers on all our exclusive offers. By the time I opened the door, there was already a crowd of people standing outside. Sheila still fought her way in to get her newspaper and browse the discounted books. She spent Christmas alone this year. It made me feel sad to think about her sitting there by herself, but she told me it was a pleasant change as she could do what she wanted. Today, she ended up buying six books along with her newspaper, using the vouchers she got for Christmas from her sister's family. I hope I still love reading when I get older.

The day passed surprisingly fast, and Jade and I were able to keep everything under control. She spotted the ring on my finger and let out a squeal of excitement. I reassured her that it wasn't a big deal. Jack had given me the ring to demonstrate his loyalty to me. She then asked why he felt a ring was necessary for that. I couldn't provide her with an answer because, truthfully, I still don't understand it myself.

Once I am out of the shower, I throw on my leggings and my mum's old football jumper and sit on my bed to text Jack.

Me: Hey, I think we need to talk.

He responds almost instantly, which makes me feel like he was thinking the same thing.

Jack: Me too. Should I come over now?

Me: I think we should go for a walk around the park.

Jack: Why? What did you say to your family?

Me: Nothing. I just think it's best we do this on neutral ground.

Jack: I will leave now. See you in ten.

There's no need for him to find out that I mentioned anything to my family yesterday. Actually, this will only fuel his anger towards me, which is something I really want to avoid right now. I make my way downstairs and slip into my khaki parka coat and trainers.

"I'm going to meet him now. I will be back soon."

My mum looks up from her book, "Ok. I love you."

"I love you too. It's going to be ok, isn't it?"

"Whatever happens, I will always be on your side. I promise."

"Thank you."

With that, I set off on my walk to the park. It's a large grassy space encircled by trees. On the far side, there are playparks for children, but I find a bench on the opposite side of the large area and tell Jack where he can meet me. I spend the next five minutes thinking about what I plan to say to him. Honestly, I have no idea what I'm going to say. I'm just hoping that the right words will come to me in the moment.

I am still deep in thought when I hear Jack, "You're still wearing the ring then. That's a good sign, I guess." He sits next to me on the bench, and I turn to face him.

"I'm not breaking up with you, Jack. I just think we need to talk about a few things."

"You have no reason to end things with me anyway. If anyone has any reason to it's me."

"You don't have any reason to."

"I do, Olivia. I told you how I felt about you going out, I told you how you weren't taking my feelings into consideration, and you still went behind my back. Then to hear you have been hanging around that bouncer, away from other people."

"It wasn't like that, Jack. I don't know who told you about it or what they told you about it, but nothing happened. He found my phone, and he returned it."

"You are completely right. Clearly, you know nothing at all. It's obvious that you had too many drinks and can't remember a thing."

"I drank as much as my friends did, and I remember the entire night. Nothing happened between Lewis and I."

SHIT! You just had to say his name, didn't you? Idiot.

"You didn't speak to him, yet you know his name? If you're going to fabricate a story, Olivia, you ought to think it over first."

"Natalia works with him. She used his name when she said hello to him, that's how I know his name. You can't call me out in front of my family like that."

"Whatever, Olivia!" He goes to stand.

"You are making me feel like I'm going crazy. This isn't fair."

"I am not responsible for your emotions, Olivia. You *are* absolutely insane."

I stand then and face him. "If you don't want me to leave the house, then that's okay, I won't go. If you don't want me to interact with other men, then fine, I won't talk to them. You have got to let me know what you expect from me, Jack. I can't just read your mind."

“I want you to apologise for going behind my back, Liv.”

“I didn’t go behind your back. What can I do to prove that to you?”

He pulls one of his hands through his hair. “We need to spend a few days apart.”

“Are you breaking up with me?” Tears start blurring my vision.

“No. I just think we both need some space to see things more clearly. I will still text and call you, but I need a few days.”

“How is this going to fix anything?”

“It’s what I need!” He yells in my face. “It’s what I want, Olivia.”

“Ok,” I say, defeated. At this point, I will do anything to make him happy. I just want us to go back to how things were. I can’t argue with him anymore. He’s right, I am crazy. I can’t tell what is real and what isn’t anymore. He is the only person who has ever tried to understand me on this deeper level, the only person who has taken on my demons as his own.

We talk for another five minutes before we part ways. My phone buzzes, and I check it.

Jack: I love you. This is for the best. We will fix us.

Chapter 23

Two days later, I wake up to a missed FaceTime call from my mum. She spent the night at the hospital with Rose. They began her induction yesterday afternoon, but they warned her that it might take a few days before anything progresses. Rob wasn't allowed to take any extra time off work, so until she goes into labor, my mum will fill in for him.

When I try to call my mum back, but she doesn't answer so I fire her a text instead.

Me: Everything ok?

While waiting for her to return my call, I start browsing through Facebook. Within moments, my newsfeed is inundated with posts from family members. I've been so preoccupied with everything happening in my life that I completely forgot what day it is. The posts are emotional, filled with images of my grandad, from his younger years to just before he passed. My mum has already switched her profile picture to one of him. A photo of him receiving medals for his service. As I like the photo, she calls me back.

"Hello," I say.

"Hi," I can hear the smile on her face just by the tone of her voice.

"She has had her, hasn't she?"

"At eight this morning."

I start to cry right away. I can hear my mum do the same on the other end of the phone. Our precious baby girl is officially part of this world. Born on one of the most important days for our family, as if our grandad sent her to us.

"I am on my way home now to shower, and then we can go back up together."

"Ok. I will have a shower now."

My mum hangs up the phone, and I find myself sobbing uncontrollably. I'm filled with immense pride for my sister. She is going to be the best mother imaginable. A small part of me feels a pang of jealousy. At this moment, I am unsure if I will ever be as lucky as she is. Jack promised to text and call, but since that last message after we parted ways, I haven't heard from him. When I finally pull myself together, I rush to the shower and have the world's fastest wash. Once I'm out, I start writing the card I purchased for her months ago. I wrap the presents and put them into a bag, and then I sit and wait for my mum to come home.

The moment I hear her key turn in the lock downstairs, I sprint out of my room and hurry halfway down the stairs. A single look at each other, and we are both crying again. My mum recounts the birth story as we drive to the hospital. Rose was amazing. Everything happened so quickly that Rob almost missed it. She told me they had chosen a name, but they wanted to wait for us to get there before revealing it. Even though she was born early, she is still a healthy weight. Both of them are recovering well from the birth.

When we get onto the ward, butterflies swarm in my stomach. I'm nervous. I'm not entirely sure why, but I am. We round a corner, and my mum opens the curtain to where my sister is sat, holding her precious little girl.

She is the most adorable little girl I have ever encountered. She is so petite that she barely covers my sister's forearm. Her head is covered with a small amount of mousy blonde hair, she has her mother's sweet little button nose and her dad's full lips. They have her in a white babygrow with small pink flowers scattered throughout. Tears fall from my eyes without any struggle. She is simply perfect.

"Hey Auntie Liv, want to hold me?" My sister asks me, in a baby voice.

She looks absolutely radiant, especially considering she gave birth just hours ago. Freshly showered and dressed in cozy PJs paired with a vibrant pink dressing gown. Amazingly, she doesn't even look tired. Her baby bump has nearly vanished. I've heard of women bouncing back, but honestly? Can it really happen this quickly?

"Of course," I say through my tears.

I sit down on the chair beside the bed, and Rose hands her over to me.

"Watch her head," she adjusts my arms, so they are in the correct position. "Yeah, just like that."

Seeing her from a distance is one thing, but up close, she takes my breath away. I wrap her tiny fingers around one of mine. "Hello, you. I have been waiting to meet you for a while now." She makes small, squeaky noises as I rub her cheek with my thumb.

"So, you want to know her name?" Rob asks us.

"Go on then," my mum says to him.

He looks to my sister, who gives him a nod of approval. "Grace."

"I love it." My mum squeals, clapping her hands together.

"Hello, Grace," I whisper to her. "I'm your auntie Liv."

The midwife comes around a few hours after we get there to tell Rose they're just finishing off the discharge paperwork, and then they can go home. Rob feels uncomfortable driving home with his new bundle of joy, so my mum has offered to take all of us girls whilst he drives their car home himself.

Whilst we're getting packed up and ready to go, Rose excuses herself to go and get changed into a comfortable outfit to wear home. Rob lets out a big sigh and holds his head in his hands.

"You, ok?" I ask him, placing a hand on his lower back.

"It's just crazy, isn't it? I can't believe she is actually here."

"You will forever be outnumbered by women now." I joke with him.

"I don't know how I will ever survive with a mini-Rose in the house."

"You'll smash it. It will come naturally after a few days, and then you will feel silly for ever stressing over it. You will both be amazing parents."

He gives me a small smile before shaking his head and blinking his tears back. "Right. I will take these bags down now and come back up."

By the time we are all buckled into the car, it's already four in the evening. My mum and I decided that once we've got Rose, Rob, and Grace home, we will order a takeaway and spend the evening watching films together. She drives slower than I have ever known her to. She says it's because she has precious cargo in the back. I don't think I could ever drive a car with a newborn baby in the back, it is way too much responsibility for me. Rose sits in the back in the middle seat so she can keep an eye on Grace.

We stay at Rose's for an hour to make sure they are settled in before we head home.

"What a day," my mum says as we walk through the front door.

"It's definitely one I will remember for a long time." I kick my shoes off and head for the sofa. "When will Dad get to meet her?"

"He said he's going to pop in when he's on his way back from golf."

"He is going to be so obsessed," I laugh. "Her being born today certainly makes me feel like this day will be easier for us now."

"Of course it will. We have something to celebrate. It will always be a sad day, but it'll be less sad now."

"I miss him."

"Don't we all? Now, what are we having for dinner?" She asks as she scrolls through her phone. "Chinese? Indian?"

"Indian sounds good."

"I will be picking the films this time, by the way," she adds. "The last two times I have let you pick, I've gone to bed in tears."

"They were good films!" I throw a pillow at her.

The last film I made her watch with me was Me Before You. I knew it was going to be sad, but I never thought it would be as sad as it was. I can't remember the last time we sat down and did something, just the two of us. It must have been before I got with Jack. Whenever it was just the two of us at home we would have nights like this, just cuddling up on the sofa watching films and filling our faces. I've missed it.

We spend the rest of the night watching my mum's film of choice, filling our bellies with good Indian food, and laughing about old memories.

I text Jack before I go to bed to let him know that Rose has had the baby, I doubt I will hear back from him, but I don't want him missing out on the big news. He was the one that came shopping with me when we found out she was having a girl, he was excited to become an uncle. *I wonder if he still is.*

Chapter 24

The next few days are spent at Rose's house, helping her and Rob in any way that we can. I've tried contacting Jack a few more times, but I've still had no response. I've decided that as its New Year's Eve, I'll invite my friends over. Jack and I were supposed to be spending it together, we had plans to book a short getaway. I'm guessing as I haven't heard from him, that he no longer plans on seeing in the New Year with me. My mum and dad will spend the night at Rose's house. As Natalia is back from visiting her boyfriend now, I know she could use the girl time.

Me: Hello, Charlies Angels. Do you want to come over tonight?

Nat: You literally read my mind.

Lily: YES PLEASE!!

Me: A cosy night, though. We can walk to the shop and get some snacks and something to drink.

Nat: I got a bottle of gin for Christmas. I will bring that.

Lily: Can we drink the gin before we go to the shop? I can't walk around town and see all the happy couples sober.

Nat: That might just be the best thing that has ever left your mouth.

Me: You two are a nightmare. Come whenever.

I spend the next hour making sure the house is clean and tidy. Somehow, I've managed to drag my mattress down the stairs and make a cosy little set-up on the living room floor. A night with my girls at home is exactly what I need to take my mind off of things.

“He was a nightmare when I was there. He literally went through my phone because he thought I was cheating on him,” Nat says to us as she finishes her second glass of gin.

“Maybe he’s just being paranoid because he is doing something he shouldn’t,” Lily adds too honestly.

“LILY!” I give her leg a playful smack.

“What? A man with something to hide acts suspiciously.”

“She isn’t wrong, Liv. I do think he’s doing something behind my back again. I have been thinking about moving in with him though.”

“What?” Lily and I exclaim in perfect harmony.

“Just to work on our relationship,” Nat says, topping off her glass.

“What if he has done something, though? Would you want to stay there with him knowing that? Would you even want to be with him?” Lily snatches the gin off of her to refill her own glass.

“I haven’t really thought that far ahead yet.”

I pour myself another glass before saying, "You can’t just bail on your life here. Not when you’re not even sure what he’s up to."

For the next hour, we chat about our Christmas days. I choose to withhold some details about my own. They’re aware that Jack and I had an argument in front of my family, and that he decided we needed to have space from each other, but I’m still keeping the details of the argument to myself. They already thought he was overreacting the first time he encountered Lewis, they don’t need to know he is the reason he needs space from me now. When the gin bottle runs dry, we agree to brave the cold winter air and take the twenty-minute stroll to the nearest store. My phone buzzes as we leave the house.

Mum: We will be heading back soon.

My mum and dad being at home will not change our plans for the night. They pretty much adopted my friends when they started spending so much time here. When we get ready for most nights out, we will sit downstairs with them for a good thirty minutes before we leave the house.

I let my friends know that they're coming home early, and they've decided we should buy even more food and drink so that they can join us.

"Is that Jack?" Nat whispers to me.

We all stand still in the street, observing the three figures who have just left the bar in front of us. So, he is alive after all. He's just opting to ignore my existence.

"It doesn't matter. Let's go," Lily says as she drags us around the corner out of view.

"What the hell, Lil!" I shout at her.

"Olivia, you haven't heard from him in days. He's clearly been out drinking, so now is not the right time to approach him." She runs a hand through her hair. "Can we please just go to the shop and get what we need."

"I am definitely going to need another drink if we're going to have to deal with him," Nat pats my shoulder and turns to walk away.

"What's that supposed to mean?" I ask my friends as I follow behind them, looking over my shoulder just in case I see Jack again.

"We love you, Liv, but things aren't good with the two of you. We see the way he acts when you're together, and it isn't healthy. He said he needed some time apart, so maybe it's better for you to give him what he needs." Nat links her arm with mine.

"I just want to ask him why he hasn't responded to my messages, that's all. He said we could still talk to each other, but he's just been ignoring me."

Lily lets out a big sigh. "Look, if we see him on the way back from the shop then I give you permission to approach him. We will stay out of sight first, and you can call his phone. If he pulls it out and doesn't answer, then we know he is ignoring you. You don't know whether his phone is broken or not."

"Sounds like a good plan to me," Nat adds

"Ugh. Fine. I hate it when you two are right."

My friends chuckle and we make it to the shop without seeing him again. We grab a basket and walk down the snack aisle, picking up basically one of everything. Usually, I'm a savoury kind of girl, but tonight, I need all the sugar I can get my hands on. When we get to the alcohol aisle, we spend a good ten minutes arguing over what drink to buy. In the end, we buy three different drinks: wine, vodka, and gin.

I'm trying to be in the moment, but now that I've seen him, I can't stop thinking about how he has been ignoring me. My brain starts overthinking like it does best. I have done so well over these last few days, keeping myself distracted with my family, but now all I want to do is to go to him. I miss him. I miss the way he holds me, the way he kisses me, the way he makes me feel safe. He accepted me with all of my flaws, and he tried to make me a better person. Without him, I feel lost. I feel like I have no idea who the hell I am.

We pay for our small shopping haul and make our way back out into the brisk winter air. I feel sick to my stomach. What if when I see him, he doesn't want to see me? We promised each other forever, but lately, it feels like forever is impossible.

"We could get a taxi back," Lily says to me.

"No. I need to do this." I look at my oldest friend with tears filling my eyes. "I have to know what's going on."

"We will be with you every step of the way, Liv. You know that right? No matter what. We will always have each other." Nat squeezes my shoulder.

A sob leaves my body, and my friends hold me in their arms. I promised myself I wouldn't let a man make me feel this way again, like I'm not worthy of being loved. My mum raised me to be an independent woman, and I feel like I'm letting her down by being so caught up in a man. But it isn't Jack's fault. It's mine. I did this. *I* am the broken one, the one that makes loving me a chore. I don't deserve the friends I have, I don't deserve the family I have, and I most definitely do not deserve the man who has done everything in his power to fix me.

I'm not sure how long we're stood there in the street holding each other, but once I have cried myself to exhaustion, I wiggle free of their hold.

"Come on. Let's just get it over with, shall we?" I wipe the tears from my cheeks and hold both of my arms out so they can each link one.

We head back to the location where we last laid eyes on Jack. Lily sneaks a look through the bar window, searching for any sign of his return. When she nods, I feel my breath catch in my throat. This is it. I shut my eyes and take a deep breath before pulling my phone from my coat pocket. Nat's hand on my lower back provides comfort, reminding me of her earlier words.

"Shit!" Lily shouts.

"What?" I glare at my friend.

"He's coming out to smoke. Get back around the corner. Quickly." She pushes us around the corner, making sure we're not seen.

Standing outside the pub, Jack, Daisy, and Dylan are unaware as Nat peeks around the corner. She discreetly gives me a thumbs up behind her back, and I make the call. I'm not surprised when it rings and goes to voicemail. Hearing his voicemail message has become a part of my daily routine. Yet, the nausea returns, as Nat is now the only one who knows the truth. Is he ignoring me on purpose? Or is his phone broken?

I wait for what feels like an eternity for her to turn around and face me. When she does, I can tell what the answer is before she even opens her mouth. My legs suddenly feel weak, and Lily has to lunge to grab me before I fall to the ground.

My head is filled with chaotic thoughts again, and they're all negative. I make an effort to yell for Nat, but my voice fails me, and I can only observe as she turns the corner and strides towards the man, I have given my all to.

As he comes around the corner, his friends following closely behind, I have found the will to stand. Lily and I haven't exchanged any words, but she did open the bottle of wine I bought for myself and allowed me to take a substantial sip from it.

"What do you want, Olivia?" Jack says as a way of greeting me. "I thought I made it clear I needed space from you. I told you not to contact me."

I feel numb. I feel nothing.

He continues speaking when I choose to ignore him, "As if you're out as well. You promised me you wouldn't go out anymore, especially with these two."

"She isn't out," Nat says from behind him. "We went to the shop to buy food and drink to spend the night inside, as per your request. Or do you expect her to stay locked inside starving to death instead?"

"She shouldn't be anywhere near you." He turns to her. "You two only make things worse."

"WORSE?" Natalia is shouting at him now. "How could we possibly make this any worse for her? You have manipulated her so badly she doesn't even know who she is anymore. You are a fucking narcissist, Jack. The right thing for you do is to let her go."

"If anyone is in the wrong here, it's her." He gets in her face. "She's the one making shit up in that fucked little head of hers. I dread to think of the lies she has told you."

"She doesn't have to tell us anything," Lily finally speaks. "We can see it all ourselves. We have eyes, Jack. Your behaviour is completely unacceptable. Olivia deserves better than this and you know that. Natalia is right, you need to let her go, let her move on from you and this relationship."

I wish the ground would just swallow me whole. This was not supposed to happen. Everything is ruined now. He'll never forgive me now my friends are involved. Lily is right. I haven't told my friends anything, but that's because Jack is also right. I don't know what the truth is and what's a lie anymore. My head is in a constant battle with itself.

"Really, Olivia!" He turns to me. "You are really going to let them speak to me like this!" He's yelling in my face now. "Do you not care about this relationship at all?" He grabs my arm and violently shakes my body. "Wake up Olivia, these two are bad for you. How many times have I told you that they've never wanted us to be together. They will do anything to ruin what we have."

Daisy is hot on Jack's heels. "Come on, Jack. We should just get back inside." She puts her hand on his arm and turns him around.

"Wait!" I manage to say.

He turns to face me, and as I walk the five steps toward him, I notice that recognisable look in his eye. The one that used to be foreign to me. He stands completely still while I reach into his jeans pocket to pull out his wallet. My eyes remain locked on his as I open it and search through until I find what I'm looking for. My hands are remarkably steady as I raise the small bag of white powder between us.

"I don't know who you are anymore." I stay looking into those now vacant eyes that I once fell in love with. "You're not the man that I fell in love with. It isn't me that's changed, Jack, it's you." I drop the small bag of powder and his wallet to the floor and push past him.

"Where the fuck do you think you're going?" He grabs my arm again.

"Home Jack. Home to spend my night with the people that really appreciate me." I throw his words from Christmas Day back in his face. "Now let me go before I scream."

"You are nothing without me." He says quietly, just for me to hear. "No one else is going to want you. Even your own dad didn't want you."

My head turns to face him at an extremely slow pace. "You did this to me." I shake off his hold. "When you're ready to work on our relationship, you know where to find me. Until then I suggest you leave me the hell alone."

"That isn't how this works, Olivia and you know it. You'll come back, and when you do, be prepared to beg."

Lily links my arm and drags me away from him and towards Nat. I feel like I just had an outer body experience, I have never stuck up for myself the way I did just then, I can feel the adrenaline surging in my veins. Time and time again people have been able to walk all over me. As I said before, everyone has a breaking point. My friends hold tightly onto my arms, and we walk in silence until we make it around the corner.

“I’m so proud of you, Liv.” Nat whispers into the darkness.

“We both are.” Lily rests her head on my shoulder.

We then hear Daisy’s blood-curdling scream, and we all stop in our tracks.

“Go back to mine.” I say to my friends, “I’ll meet you back there.”

They choose not to argue with me. They look at each other briefly before nodding and walking away. Leaving me to clean up whatever mess he has made…again.

Chapter 25

Before I turn the corner, I take a deep and steady breath, preparing myself mentally for whatever it is I'm about to see. Daisy is bent down, rubbing Jack's back, and Dylan has his hands on top of his head, whilst pacing up and down the street by the time I come up behind them. I didn't need to see what happened, I know now what this man is capable of.

"Get up," I say from behind them, making Daisy jump up and move out of the way.

Jack stands slowly and turns to me, holding his hand. I can see the blood pouring from his knuckles, the tears lining his eyes. *Who would punch a brick wall? I mean, really? Again? He didn't win that fight the first time, why on earth would you attempt it again?*

"Come on," I hold my hand out to him, my voice void of any emotion. "You can come back with me, and I'll clean your hand up."

Even though I'm so mad at him right now, it makes my heart ache to see him hurt. It isn't just him, it's anybody who is hurting, the empath in me can't help herself.

"You don't have to go, Jack," Daisy says, grabbing his arm. "Stay here with us, I can help you."

"It's fine. I'll be back in a bit, I just need to get this all sorted out first." He keeps his eyes locked on mine. I'm not sure at this moment in time whether he is on about his hand or me. He knows he can't go back to his mother's house on drugs. She would take one look at him and kick him to the curb. No bar will let him inside with his knuckles bruised and bloody either. His only option is to go with me.

We walk in silence until we get to my front door. "Wait here," I say to him. Thankfully, he does as I ask.

As I enter my house, I find my friends and parents sitting at the kitchen table. They stop their conversation as I enter the room. My mum is the only one who looks up at me. I know my friends would have filled her in on the events that have happened, so I don't bother explaining it all.

"He punched a wall. I need to clean his hand up."

She lets out a big sigh and rubs her forehead with her right hand. "You can take him upstairs. I don't want to see him right now."

I nod and turn back towards the front door. When I get him in my upstairs bathroom, he finally breaks the silence between us.

"I'm sorry."

"It's fine," I say to him as I fill the sink with warm water. I turn to get a flannel from the airing cupboard, and he grabs hold of my hip. The warmth of his touch makes butterflies swarm in my stomach. *My traitorous body.*

"I mean it, Olivia. I am so sorry." He looks into my eyes, and I find myself searching him for any sign of the man I love, but he isn't there.

"When you're sober and say it, I might believe you." I remove his hand from my hip and continue with what I was doing.

"You can't leave me, Liv."

"Honestly, Jack, right now I don't have the energy for this conversation. I will decide what's right for me, no one can make that decision for me."

After five minutes have passed, the water in the sink is tainted red with blood. His knuckles have ceased bleeding, yet they're already bruised and significantly swollen. I continue to grip his hand, fearful that if I release it, I might never have the chance to hold it again.

"Stay here tonight," my voice comes out more unsteady than I would like it to. "If you *are* really sorry, then stay. We can talk about it all."

He snatches his hand from me and when I look up at him, any sign of apology has vanished from his face. I think he may actually be annoyed at my suggestion.

"I'm not staying here, Liv. My friends are waiting for me." He pushes to stand and shoves his way past me. "Why would I want to see the New Year in with you, after everything you've done tonight."

"Jack, please," I beg him.

"I don't want to hear it, Olivia." He runs down the stairs and pulls the front door open, letting the harsh, cold air hit me.

"I have a bad feeling about tonight." I manage to catch up with him outside my house. "Please. Please just stay."

"I have plans. I won't change them for you."

"I'm sure they'll understand. They all like us together, they'd want us to fix everything." Tears start flowing from my eyes, and in a desperate attempt to stop him from walking away, I grab his arm like he has done to me so many times before. "Please, Jack. I am begging you. Please don't go."

"I don't want to stay, Olivia!" He shouts in my face. "They may have liked the idea of us in the beginning, but then you ruined everything. Now I don't think they would care if they never saw you again."

My vision is starting to get all spotty. This can't be happening right now! Now is definitely not the time for a panic attack. I close my eyes, trying to push it away. It does nothing to ease the situation. My breathing becomes erratic, and that weight on my chest is back. The right side of my body begins to tingle and feel weak. I let go of his hand, crouching down to hold my chest with my left hand. "Don't start this shit." I think he says to me.

"Please," I say to him through my sobs. "Please," I am hit by a cold sweat coating my entire body. "Please."

"No."

At this point, I have fully lost control of both my body and my mind. My vision is back to normal, but I can barely breathe, which is making me feel faint. My head is pounding. The nausea is almost unbearable.

"Stop pretending and get up." He holds his hand out for me to take.

He doesn’t try to reassure me the way he has done countless times before. He just stands there watching me. “Help. Me.” I manage to get out.

He rolls his eyes. He genuinely rolls his eyes at me. As if I’m doing this intentionally. As if I have any say in the matter. When I come to the realisation that I will have to face this alone, I shut my eyes and envision my mum's soothing voice. I think of her until I can hear her voice echoing in my mind. She tells me how to concentrate on my breathing. I listen to her advice. I follow every step she takes me through until my breathing becomes steadier and the discomfort in my chest eases. When I finally open my eyes to glance at him, he is answering a phone call.

“I won’t be much longer,” a pause, “get me another drink,” another pause, “I will tell you when I get there,” and then he hangs up.

“Who was that?” I say as I stand again.

“None of your business.” He slides the phone back into his jeans pocket. “I have to go.”

“Jack please, I’m scared. Please just stay.”

“I don’t want to see your fucking face, Olivia!”

He pushes past me, and that’s when I see my mum stood just outside our front door. Her mouth is hanging open, and she has her right hand on her chest. She may even be crying, but I can’t see clearly through the darkness.

“You!” She shouts as she heads towards me. “You can leave your key!” I realise then she is talking to Jack behind me.

“My what?” He spins to face her.

“You heard me. You are no longer welcome in my house. Give me my key back.”

“I don’t have it with me.” He smirks at her.

Bad move buddy.

“You either give it back to me now, or I will call the police.”

"I would like to see you try. No one is going to arrest me because you want your house key back."

My eyes bulge from my head. My mum is usually a calm soul, but if you hurt her children, she will hunt you to the ends of the earth. There have been many times in my life where she has dropped everything to come and defend me and Rose.

"I'm sure they would love to hear about how you sold your car to pay off your drug debt. I also wonder if they'd search you and make you take a drug test tonight?"

"What?" I look at my mum. Now, it is my jaw on the floor.

"Oh, yeah, it was never broken. He sold it to his dealer to pay off his debt. Remember when he 'borrowed' Jordan's car to take you away? He had already sold it." She stays staring at the man in front of us, her arms crossed over her chest.

"Are you not too old to be spreading lies?" He raises his brows at her.

"Lies? Yes. The truth? No. The man you sold it to plays football with my husband," she walks two steps towards him, "Ben was more than willing to talk his ear off about it."

Ben has been a friend of my dad's for years. I say friend, but what I mean is they've played football together since they were teenagers. Outside of that time, they don't speak to each other or see each other. He works as a cleaner at one of the supermarkets in town, and I always found myself wondering how he managed to afford all his designer clothing and fancy Land Rover. Now I know. If he paid his debt off all those months ago, I wonder how much debt he's got himself into since.

Jack says nothing as he pulls his keys from his jacket pocket and takes off the one for our front door. He holds it out towards my mum, but she doesn't move. She just stands there staring at him. He drops it on the floor and turns away without saying another word.

"I'm sorry," my mum turns to me. "I am so sorry."

Then I'm crying in her arms, she runs her fingers through my hair, shushing me the way she would've done when we were children. "Come on, baby."

She lets go of me to walk over the key and pick it up. Then she takes my hand to lead me back to our house, but the nausea is too much. The anxiety has completely taken over my body and I am no longer in control. I have enough time to drop her hand and turn away from her before I throw up everywhere. I empty the entire contents of my stomach on the floor. When I'm finished, my dad comes out to us with a bucket of water to wash it away.

As I walk through the door, I notice my mattress has disappeared along with my friends. I haven't said anything in a while, but I don't need to. My mum runs her thumb over my cheek and signals with her head for me to go upstairs. I'm too tired to argue with her, so I just do as she says. When I walk into my room, I find them both in my bed. They have each helped themselves to a pair of my PJs. Lily pulls back the covers and gestures for me to get into the bed between the two of them, and I do.

As I lay there in my bed, each of my friends snuggled in close on each side of me, I think back to the events of tonight and what went so wrong.

Maybe I should have left him alone, I should have given him the space he wanted, but I'm convinced he said we could still talk to each other. I may have made that up, though. I have known Dylan and Daisy for longer than Jack has. I have spent countless nights with Daisy, either out on the town or around hers, for sleepovers with Georgia. They both just stood there and let him talk to me and my friends that way. They didn't try to intervene. In fact, they were trying to keep him away from me. *Am I the bad guy in this situation?* I search every crevasse of my mind to see if there is anything I could've done to upset either of them, but I come up empty-handed. Dylan, I can understand, but Daisy...

Was I stupid to help him? Should I have left him there bleeding in the street? I have way too much empathy. It's one of my biggest strengths but it's also my biggest weakness. I don't have it in me to leave someone who needs help. Especially when I'm so madly and deeply in love with them, no one else would have helped him the way I did.

Should I have not asked him to stay with me? Is it controlling that I did? I just wanted us to stay together tonight and work through this. Now I'm really thinking about it I'm not sure we can. I'm starting to think that too much has happened now, for us to go back to the way we were.

"I love you," I manage to say to my friends.

"I love you too," Lily whispers.

"I love you three," Nat chuckles to herself.

I know he thinks my friends are bad for me, but I can't imagine my life without them. I try to think about all the terrible things they could've done for him to think we shouldn't be friends, but the truth is, they've always been there by my side through everything. Every heartbreak, every friendship falling out, family issues, we have helped each other through it all.

"It will be ok, Liv. No matter what happens next, we will be here." Lily says into the darkness.

"I know. I just don't know if I can survive this." A single tear rolls down my cheek.

"Of course you can. You're the strongest person I know. Olivia White doesn't back down from a challenge."

"I don't know if I want to fight for it anymore."

"We can cross that bridge together if it happens."

"I thought he was different."

"We all did, babe. Don't beat yourself up over it. He fooled us all," Nat says.

Chapter 26

My alarm wakes us all up way too early the next day. I know my friends slept because I sat up listening to their snoring. I think I managed to get around two hours in total before I woke up covered in sweat and was sick again. Last night I felt a slight bit of relief when we were in bed together, like everything was going to be ok. With or without Jack, my life would be ok, I would heal. But when I woke up at three, something was different. I couldn't tell you what it was, but you know when you just have a gut feeling that something is wrong? I had that feeling, and it has stuck with me ever since.

I scan my social media, looking for Instagram and Snapchat stories from Jack, Daisy, or Dylan, but there are none.

Today is a new day, though. I try to push the feeling in my stomach aside to get ready for work.

"You two can stay here if you want to. Get some more sleep, and if you're still here when I get home from work, maybe we can get a takeaway?"

"I can stay if it's fine with your mum and dad." Lily pushes to a sitting position.

"That all sounds lovely. Now stop talking so I can get more of that sleep you spoke of," Nat says into the pillow.

I shuffle out of the bed and grab my uniform.

"I love you," I say to Lily mainly, as I am fairly sure Nat has already drifted back off to sleep in the two minutes it took me to grab what I need.

"I love you too. If you need me, just call me."

The walk to work is cold, but at least it's not raining, I tell myself. If it started raining right now, it would fully push me over the edge. I have done the best I can with my appearance today. My eyes are still puffy and swollen from crying so much, so I have added a small amount of concealer and mascara. My hair is another story, though. I've shoved it into a messy bun on top of my head. I did brush it before I put it up, so I'm taking that as a small win. My headphones are plugged into my phone, and I have Taylor Swift playing at full volume. This earns me a few strange looks from the older people out walking their dogs. There's a Taylor Swift song for every occasion, no one can tell me any different. Sad? Taylor. Happy? Taylor. Revenge mode? Taylor.

Luckily for me, as its New Year's Day, I only see a handful of dog walkers on the way down to the shop. Everyone my age will still be in bed with a killer hangover. Some may even still be up partying. I wonder if Jack is. I imagine after last night he probably went back out and consumed way too much alcohol.

That feeling in my stomach comes back again as I walk through the shop to the staff room. It's Jade's day off today, which is actually quite gutting. I'm not as close to the other girls as I am to Jade. But then again, it may be nice to get through this shift without having to talk about what happened last night. Maggie should be here shortly after I open up so I can hide in a corner somewhere away from socialisation.

As I open up, Sheila is there, like she is every other day. "You look like you had a rough night dear?" She says to me as she waddles in with her trolley.

"Something like that."

"Well, I can tell you've been crying," she eyes me over her glasses, "it better not be that boy of yours, I'm hoping you've just had too much to drink."

She passes me her paper, and I chuckle at her. "Unfortunately, it's all because of him."

As I pass her paper back over the till to her, she holds my hand. "Dear, do not let a man make you feel this way. You are too young to be tied down in an unhappy relationship. Too beautiful to waste your tears on a man who does not see what he has. These are your best years, live them to the fullest."

I wipe a stray tear from my cheek and smile at her, "Thank you."

"Don't thank me. Life is too short. Do not waste it on him."

With that, she turns and leaves. Old people always know the right thing to say. They have the life experience, I guess. I often forget she was young once, she would have been through similar things. You never think about that. She's right, I do deserve to be treated better than I have been.

I serve a few more customers before Maggie comes in. I say Happy New Year to them all, and even though my New Year has been anything but happy, I offer them all my best fake smile. You never know what someone else might be going through. It may be the only time they have a positive conversation today. The feeling in my stomach has disappeared now I'm distracted with work. I still have a headache, from all of the crying and lack of sleep, but I can live with that.

At around eleven, I'm busy down the back end of the store, reshelving all of our stationery. New Year, new display. I am surrounded by various folders when I hear someone shout down the front of the store. "Where is she!"

Whoever it is has clearly been running. I can hear their heavy breathing from here.

"Maggie, for god sake where is she? I do not care about what you got up to last night. Where is she? Where is Olivia?" The voice is familiar now. It's Jade.

"Thank you. That wasn't hard was it! Happy New Year to you and all that jazz."

I hear her running up to the back of the store. I try to keep myself busy, acting like I didn't just hear her come charging in. I don't know what it is that she wants, but that feeling in my stomach is back with a vengeance.

"Get out the back now," Jade says as a way of greeting me.

"Good morning to you, too." I spot her uniform. "You do know today is your day off, right?"

"Not anymore, it isn't. Out the back. Now."

"I am in the middle of something right now. Can it wait until I'm done?" I gesture to the mess on the floor around me.

"Does this look like the face of someone who has all the time in the world?" She glares at me.

"I don't think you want me to answer that."

"Olivia Chloe White. Do not make me drag you out by your hair."

At this point, several of the customers in the store are staring at us both. There's nothing I would love more than to act out an episode of a soap opera on the shop floor with her, just to avoid whatever it is she so desperately has to tell me, but if my boss catches wind of us fighting on the shop floor, we will probably both be fired. Reluctantly, I wave my hand in front of her and gesture her to the door that takes us to the staff room. I barely have time to sit at the desk before she starts.

"Why have you not answered your phone?" She glares at me.

"You sound like Jack." The joke falls on death ears. "Jesus, mum, calm down. I'm working. I was on my own until Maggie got here, and I've been busy since. I mean you saw the state of the floor out there."

"It's not the time for jokes, Liv. I mean it. When did you last hear from Jack?"

I rest my elbows on the desk and hang my head in my hands. How silly was I to think I could go a whole day without having to talk about this? News in this town travels fast, but how the hell does Jade know anything about it?

"Does it matter, Jade? I really don't have the energy to talk about any of it."

She sits in the chair next to me and puts her hand on my knee. "I need to know, Liv."

I let out a grunt and turn to face her. "Last night. I saw him in town, he punched a wall, I took him home and patched him up. I then begged him to stay with me because I had a terrible feeling about him going out. He left me on the street crying in my mum's arms before I threw up everywhere. Are you happy now?"

"Jesus, really?" She shakes her head. "But no. No, I'm obviously not happy. I don't want to be the one to have this conversation with you, but apparently no one else is going to."

My palms become clammy, my mouth is drier than the Sahara Desert, and that feeling in my stomach threatens to make me sick again. "What conversation?"

"Before I tell you, I don't know how true it is. I heard it from someone he was with last night, but I have no reason not to believe him."

"For god sake, Jade, spit it out."

"I tried to warn you about him, Liv. I tried my hardest to get you to see what he is really like." She takes a deep breath. "This isn't fair, you don't deserve any of this. You are the kindest, most loving person I have ever met. None of this is your fault, you have to know that before I say anything."

"Jade, I know you know one of my love languages is words of affirmation, and I appreciate the nice things you've said, but I told you I don't have the energy for this today. Please, whatever it is, just tell me."

"Jack took Daisy home with him last night."

That feeling of dread peaks, the feeling I have had since last night, when I begged him to stay with me. That feeling that came back in the early hours of this morning, making me sick again, and then again just five minutes ago when she came to find me. I barely make it to the toilet before I'm sick again. I'm surprised though because I thought I would be empty by now, I have no idea how it's still coming up. Jade knocks before coming in and sitting beside me on the toilet floor. "Who did you hear it from?"

"Liv, I don't know for sure if anything happened."

“Jade!” I turn to look at her, still hanging over the toilet. I speak slowly. “Who. Did. You. Hear. It. From?”

She looks down at her lap. Suddenly, her nails become the most interesting thing in the world. “Dylan.”

I push myself back from the toilet and lean against the wall. Dylan would have no reason to lie to Jade. I look at the ring on my finger, the ring he gave me as he promised he would be faithful to me. My entire relationship has been a lie. I wish I could feel something, pain, anger, anything, but I am numb again. I have no fight left in me.

“I came in so you could go home and deal with it. You don’t have to say anything to Cindy. She’s off today anyway, so I can cover for you. I am so sorry, Liv.”

“Just stop. Please just stop.” I look into her sad eyes. “I am so sick of people telling me they are sorry for his actions.”

“Please don’t be mad at me. I didn’t want to have to tell you, but I didn’t think he would.”

“I need to go.” I stand and look back at her over my shoulder. “Thank you.”

“Liv!” She shouts after me. “I meant everything I said to you. You deserve better than this.”

“I know.”

With that, I gather my things and make my way to the front of the store. I tell Maggie I have to leave for a family emergency. My mum couldn’t get hold of me, so she contacted Jade thinking she was working today. Jade backs up my story and ushers me out of the store.

The walk home isn’t long enough for me to think about what I’m going to do next. The second I walk through the door, everyone in that house is going to know something is up. I debate just sitting on the doorstep and ignoring my problems, hoping they will just go away.

How could he do this to me? He told me he would never cheat on me, he said he knows how it feels, and he would never wish that pain on someone else. He said so many things to me during our time together, how many of them were true?

My brain was already confused. Now, it has just malfunctioned.

As I thought, when I walk through the door, my parents and friends stop watching TV and laughing together and stare at me. All of the emotions I managed to hold back whilst I was at work all come out. I drop to my knees in the living room and hold my head in my hands. Each sob leaves me breathless. My heart is breaking into thousands of tiny little pieces. No, it has shattered, and it will never be mended. Nothing and no one can fix this.

"What happened?" My mum is on her knees in front of me. She pulls my hands from my face and holds my head in her hands, so I am forced to look up at her. "What did he do?"

"He took Daisy home," the words fall out of my mouth with such ease. That filter between my head and my mouth has well and truly been broken, probably from all the lies I have had to tell over these last few months.

I hear the gasps from my friends in the background, but I am stuck looking into my mum's eyes. I feel like I'm seven years old again, begging her to let me move school, to get me away from the people who hurt me so badly. Even I know deep down this is not something that my mum can fix.

"Lee," she calls out to my dad, but she keeps her eyes locked on mine.

"What do you need?" He asks, coming over to us. He kneels next to my mum and puts his hand on my shoulder.

"Bags." She breaks eye contact to look at her husband. "Get the big Ikea bag."

With a nod he gives my shoulder a squeeze and starts hunting for the world's biggest bag.

"Girls," she looks over her shoulder to my friends, who are both sobbing at the sight of me. "Take her upstairs. Get her changed."

They help me up from the floor and lead me up the stairs without saying a word. Lily walks me to my bed and sits with me. She rests my head on her shoulder and holds it there with one hand. Natalia starts raiding my wardrobe for something I can wear.

"All I can find is his clothes." She sobs into her hands.

"Swap with me," Lily says. "I'll have a look." For once, Nat doesn't argue with her, and she does as she is told.

After a few minutes, she throws some clothes on the bed, a pair of leggings and my Era's Tour jumper. When I don't move, they take matters into their own hands and start stripping my uniform off of me. We have seen each other in our underwear more times than I can count. Even if we hadn't, I wouldn't care right now. I feel paralysed. Even normal actions like blinking and swallowing feel hard right now.

"I don't know what to say," Nat says.

"That's because there isn't anything to say. Please, whatever you do, do not apologise to me. I can't hear anyone else say sorry to me for his actions. I got myself into this mess."

"This isn't your fault. I promise you that."

Chapter 27

By the time the girls had got me dressed, my mum had made her way upstairs with the Ikea bag she asked my dad to find. I can see she has been crying. It hurts me when I see her sad. It isn't fair that she's sad, she has had enough sadness in her life already to last her a lifetime. My already shattered heart aches for her. It's my fault she is hurting right now, I bought this man into my life, and then into my family's lives.

"Help me get all of his stuff in here," my mum holds her hand out for me to take.

I take it and sit on the floor next to her. My friends take a seat on my bed next to each other and watch silently. I rummage through the drawers and wardrobe and hand my mum all of his belongings, she is usually anal when it comes to folding clothes, so they don't get creases, but today she just shoves it in the bag all screwed up. When we're finished getting all of his clothes together, I pick up the loose things from around my room. A charger, a pair of trainers, one of his aftershaves. Whilst I gather the things in the bathroom, my mum rummages through our dirty wash basket for any of his clothes still waiting to be washed. I hold his shower gel in my hand, and the pain hits me like a bus. I may never smell him again, I may never hold him again. Before I take it back into my room, I open the lid and take a big inhale of it. The citrus and sandalwood notes fill my nose, and for just a second, my heart doesn't hurt.

When all of his things are packed in a bag, my friends say goodbye to me. They think it's best I deal with this with my family. I know they're right, but I still wish they could be here when I get home. It's the thought of being alone that scares me the most.

My mum pulls her car up to the car park that's closest to his house.

"Ready?" She looks over at me.

I take a deep breath in and nod. With that, we get out of the car. I can't feel how cold it is, but I know it must be cold because my mum shivers as she throws on her coat. She leads the way up to his parents' house. I follow closely behind her, wishing we could drag this out, so I don't have to face him so quickly. *What will I even say to him?*

As my mum knocks on their front door, I hear his mum, "Jack. She's here."

She. I'm not very close with his family, mainly because he doesn't like to stay here often. He says it's too busy here and it's easier for us to stay at mine. Now I'm starting to think he just didn't want me here, he wanted to keep me away from my friends and family, so why wouldn't he want to keep me away from his. I have never argued with him about it, but it still hurts to hear her talk about me like I'm a nobody.

"Well, at least we know he's here," my mum mumbles under her breath.

We wait at his front door for over five minutes before we hear the key on the other side, I was almost ready to just leave his stuff on the doorstep and walk away. It's his younger sister Sarah who opens the door. She has a smug smile on her face, which only makes my blood boil. That's when I realise, I'm not even sad anymore. I'm just angry. Anger is the worst kind of emotion to feel, but he doesn't deserve to see how much he has hurt me, so I keep all signs of emotion off of my face.

My mum pushes past Sarah and walks through their small entry hall into the open-plan kitchen-dining room. To the left of the front door is a door to the front room, and I think I see movement out of the corner of my eye, but I don't dare to go and investigate, so I follow my mum. Jack's mother is stood on the other side of the table, but she doesn't look at me. She only watches my mother as she empties the bag onto the table.

"Here are all of Jack's belongings. He will not be keeping my bag." My mum folds the bag up and sticks it under her arm. "Well," she looks to his mother now. "Where is he?"

She breaks eye contact with my mum to look down at her incredibly interesting slippers. "He's still in bed. He will be down in a minute."

I faintly hear the front door close and turn quick enough to see Sarah duck into the front room away from the commotion.

"Are you proud of him?" My mum asks. "Are you ok with his behaviour?"

"I don't know anything," she says quietly.

"You allowed this to happen under your roof. What does that say about your parenting? Do you know all of the things your son has been up to?"

She opens her mouth to say something but quickly closes it again as Jack comes down the stairs. It's so silent you could hear a pin drop. My first thought when I look at him is that he looks tired. His eyes are sunken, and he has red rings under them. His stubble is just a little bit too long, and his hair is a mess. He is wearing a black slim-fit T-shirt paired with some skinny grey jogging bottoms. At least he looks like he's paying for the amount of alcohol and drugs he consumed last night.

"There's all of your stuff. You will not step foot back in my house ever again." My mum says to him.

"I am not talking to you about this."

"It isn't me I want you to speak to. It's my daughter." She points at me, "I hope it was worth it, Jack."

"If Olivia wants to talk to me, I'll talk to her outside."

She looks at me, and I nod to her. "I'll be at home. Call me when you're done and I'll pick you up. I'm only a text away if you need me."

Jack waits for her to leave before he finds his trainers and a hoodie to wear. "Walk with me," he holds his hand out for me to take, but I walk straight past him to the front door. The last thing I want right now is for him to be touching me. He clearly hasn't showered.

We walk in silence for a few minutes before he speaks, "Talk to me, Olivia."

"I don't know what you want me to say." I stop and sit on a bench far enough away from his house so his family can't hear us.

"Anything. But please, Liv, talk to me."

"Did you sleep with her?" I ask

"Yes." He hangs his head. "It was a mistake. I didn't mean to do it."

"Was she still in there when I got there? Is she who your sister snuck out?"

"Yes."

"And what part of it was a mistake?"

"All of it, Liv. It was all one big mistake."

A small, humourless laugh leaves me. "I'm sorry. Let me get this right. You didn't mean to walk home with her and let her into your bed? You didn't mean to get naked with her? and what? It accidentally slipped in? And then you and your family didn't mean to sneak her out of your house when your girlfriend turned up?"

"It wasn't like that, Liv. I was angry with you. Things weren't good with us."

"This is my fault, is it?"

"No." He runs his good hand through his hair. "I fucked up."

"That's one word for it, yes. You promised me. You promised this wouldn't happen. You said you would never hurt me this way." Tears start to flow down my face.

"I'm sorry, Liv. I really am." He holds my left hand in his "Please, tell me what I can do."

"That's the thing, Jack. I don't think there is anything you can do. You can't take it back. You can't change what has happened. I will never trust you after this."

"So what? You're going to throw everything we have away because of one mistake?"

"I don't know," I say honestly. "It isn't just last night though, Jack. You have told so many lies, you've done so many terrible things to me. I don't recognise myself anymore."

He gets off the bench and gets on his knees in front of me. He lays his head in my lap for a minute before he looks up at me, and the tears leak from his eyes. "Please, Olivia. You can't leave me. Please don't leave me."

He is deadly serious right now. After months of trying to manipulate me and turn me against my friends and family, he is on his knees in front of me, begging for me to stay. Last night I poured my heart out to him, I begged him to stay, and he walked away from me like I was nothing. All I have wanted from him is for him to want me, for him to be scared of losing me, but it's too late. The ship has sailed. I'm too hurt.

"I don't know what I'm going to do, Jack. I need time. I need time to think it all through before I make a decision."

"Don't say that Liv. You don't need time. We love each other."

"Love isn't always enough, Jack."

"Please, Liv. Please don't shut me out."

"I need time!" I shout at him. "Just like you did. I need time."

"You don't. I can fix this. Let me fix this."

"I don't know if you can, Jack." I hold my face in my hands. "The lies, the cheating, the drink, the drugs. It's too much."

We stayed there on the bench, talking for another two hours. I lost count of how many times Jack apologised for his actions. He finally caved and said it was ok for me to have some time to think things through. We cried on each other, we laughed, we cried some more. I made him call Jordan so he could take him to the hospital for his hand. When it was time for us to part ways, I took the ring off of my finger and gave it back to him. He tried to fight it and told me I should keep it, but I told him it lost its value when he did what he did. I also don't want the reminder on my finger every day.

My mum picked me up when we were finished talking, I know she isn't happy with my decision not to end things, but I don't want to make a decision that could be the wrong one. He has done a lot of bad things, but he has also been the one to make me feel safe and cared for. We have dinner together as a family and I stay sitting downstairs with them for a while after. When I start to get tired, I excuse myself.

Chapter 28

After an hour of tossing and turning in my bed, I give up trying to fall asleep and brave a look at my phone for the first time since this morning. I check in with Lily and Nat, and I tell them what happened. I told them I didn't end things because I didn't want to make any rash decisions.

Nat: It might be for the best. At least with the time to yourself you can think about it, without him having an input.

Lily: I agree! Definitely the right decision.

Lily: If you need us, give us a call!

It's such a strange feeling. I'm so angry at Jack for what he's done, but Daisy, I feel nothing. I might be slightly disappointed, but that's it. If she thinks it's ok to do that type of thing to someone who she calls her 'best friend,' then I don't want to be her friend anymore. Things start to make much more sense to me now. She was the one who told Jack that I was with Lewis that night, the gentle way she was touching him and trying to keep him from going with me last night.

My mind starts spinning when I think back to all the things that have happened and how she might be involved. I try to message Georgia, to make sure everything is still ok between the two of us.

Me: Hey, I am sure you have heard what has happened by now. I just wanted to check we were still ok. Love you.

MESSAGE FAILED TO SEND

Weird.

I decide to check her Facebook. If her phone was broken, she would write a status about it. Her phone is her lifeline. She couldn't survive without it. When I search her name, nothing comes up. Next, I try Daisy, but still nothing. I work my way through the rest of our small friendship group. It's the same with each of them. *Blocked.* They have blocked me.

I go through all of my social media apps until I find that Georgia hasn't blocked me on Instagram yet. I instantly send her a message, before she realises and blocks me on there too.

Me: Have you blocked me?

Georgia: I don't want to argue with you, Olivia. We heard about how you've been controlling Jack. I won't be friends with someone like that.

Me: Me controlling him? He cheated on me.

Georgia: He only cheated because you made him so miserable.

Me: I did everything I could to make him happy. How about you listen to both sides of the story before you all decide that I'm the bad guy? You're meant to be my best friend, G.

Georgia: I'm not interested in you trying to brainwash me as well.

I try to respond but she blocks me before I have a chance.

I've lost everything. My relationship, my friends. Everything I have worked so hard to get. It's all gone. The fear begins to settle in at that moment. I'm all by myself. I rush to the bathroom and lock the door behind me. I sit on the floor with my head resting on my knees. I ride through the panic attack alone until the depression takes over.

For the first time in ages, I find myself not wanting to be here. I feel worse now than I did before Jack. As I reach for the razor next to the bath, I don't even think about what I'm doing. I snap it until one of the blades rests in my hand. No one would even notice if I disappeared. In fact, I'd be doing them a favor. They wouldn't have to live their lives worrying about me all the time. The girl who, no matter what, will never find happiness. They might feel sad initially, but they would quickly move on and forget about me. I press the blade against the skin of my wrist. I think I scream, but I keep going.

There's a constant pounding on the bathroom door. My mum is shouting, but I can't grasp what she's saying. The thoughts swirling in my head drown out all sound. Eventually, my dad breaks the door down.

When I see my mum's face, I drop the blade instantly. She is worth living for. She is worth fighting for.

"What are you doing?" She grabs hold of the arm covered in blood. "Baby, why?"

"I'm sorry," I say to her. "I am so sorry. I'm sorry."

"Nobody is worth this baby. Nobody." She picks me up and carries me to her bed. "You can sleep here tonight. We'll go and see the doctor tomorrow. Ok?"

"Why can't someone just make it all go away?" I sob, "Please, Mummy, please make it stop."

"If I could, I would." She runs her hands through my hair. "Don't let him do this to you."

We lay there together for a while after she has cleaned me up. When she tells me she's going to get herself a drink, I hear her in the bathroom, probably hiding all the sharp objects. I have been low before, but I've never been this low. What do I even say to the doctor?

Before I fall asleep, I reach for my phone, which my mum has plugged in beside her bed. With a steady hand, I pull Jack's text thread up and send the message that will change my life.

Me: I am so sorry, Jack, but I can't do this anymore. I love you. I will love you forever, but we're bad for each other.

Thank you for loving me and showing me that there is a life out there that's worth living. I'm so sorry that the life I want to live is not a life with you. Things have been bad for such a long time now that I don't see us getting back to what we were before. I wish you the best in life, I truly do. I really hope you find a girl one day who can love you the way you want to be loved. She unfortunately, isn't me.

I need this time to myself now. I need to heal from all the hurt you have inflicted on me. I will never forget all of the good times we spent together.

I said forever, and I meant it, but our forever will have to be spent apart.

I lock my phone and lay it back on the bedside table. Part of me already feels better. It's going to be scary starting over, but it will be worth it.

Tomorrow is a new day.

Chapter 29

The next day, my mum wakes me up with a lovely breakfast in bed. She offers me a cup of coffee in one of my dad's Sports Direct mugs, which is nearly a jug of coffee, and has made pancakes covered in sugar.

"We have to be at the doctors in forty-five minutes," she says to me, planting a kiss on the top of my head. "I'm going to have a quick shower first."

"Thank you," I give her a small smile.

While enjoying my breakfast, the temptation to check my phone is too strong to resist. I grab it and take a deep breath as I look at the screen. There are several text messages and missed calls from Jack, but instead of opening them, I delete them. I said everything I needed to say. I don't want to hear what he has to say. I want to avoid being swayed by his words. I need to focus on my own growth. I don't want to be with another man, ever.

My cat jumps up onto the bed and presses his head against mine, his unique way of saying hello. He really can pick up on my emotions. I believe he knows me better than I know myself somedays. I place my phone down and bring him up onto my chest, we lay here together for five minutes until my mum steps out of the shower. Then, I know that I can't delay getting ready any longer.

I opt for a pair of navy-blue skinny jeans today, pairing them with a cropped beige jumper. Instead of throwing my hair up on top of my head, I give it a quick once over with a pair of straighteners, then part it into a half-up, half-down hairstyle. I've decided against makeup today, even though I wouldn't have time to do it anyway. For someone who has spent the last two days doing nothing but crying and throwing up, I don't think I look too bad.

We walk to the doctors as it's just up the hill from my mum's house. I think she can tell that I feel nervous, but she doesn't say anything to me. She's good like that. She knows exactly what to say and when to say it.

Our surgery was refurbished recently, and it now has two floors. The ground floor is home to the reception desk, and a large waiting area. It's filled with a number of different chairs, all matching in colour, but different in style. The grey chairs are all spread out evenly across the white tiled floor, just as they were during the pandemic. Down here there are several rooms, as far as I'm aware they're used for nurse appointments. Upstairs the décor is very much the same as the lower level, but there are large windows across one wall, letting the light pour in. The rooms up there are for appointments to see the doctor.

Once we have checked in at the reception desk, we are sent upstairs. We're not waiting in the waiting room for exceptionally long when a blonde-haired doctor pokes her head out. "Olivia White, please."

My mum takes my hand in hers and leads me through the door. She takes a seat near the door leaving me to sit in the one directly in front of the doctor.

"Hi, Olivia. My name is Doctor Jones. How can I help you today?"

"Umm," I look to my mum, who gives me a reassuring nod. "I'm not doing so well mentally."

"Ok, that's fine. I can definitely help you with that today. Are you happy talking about everything in front of your mum?"

"Yes. I wouldn't be able to do it without her here."

"Perfect. Why don't you start by telling me how long you have been struggling for?"

A big sigh leaves my body, "A while. A few months even."

"Has something happened in your life that could be making you feel this way?"

"A lot of things," I shake my head. "I wouldn't know where to start."

"Let's start at the beginning," she gives me a warm smile.

I spend the next twenty minutes telling her about my background, everything from being bullied, to all of the stuff we went through with my dad. They've heard me talk about this before, but I don't think I've ever been this honest with them. I then get onto the topic of Jack. I mention his anger and very specifically him hitting walls out of anger. I tell her about him not wanting me to go out with my friends, not wanting me to go and see my sick nan in the hospital, but that it was ok for him to go out and do as he pleased. I tell her about the cheating. I leave out all of the stuff about the drugs and the fact he had sex with me against my will. I don't want him to get arrested, and I'm also not ready to admit these things to my mum. I finish it off by telling her I self-harmed. It's not the first time I've done it, but it's the first time anyone knows about it.

"You have tried therapy before?" She quickly scans my medical record on her screen.

"Yes. I've done a few of the toolkits."

"I think we need something more than that. Perhaps some CBT would be helpful. I also want to sign you off from work for a few weeks. Does that sound ok to you?"

"Sign me off?" I frown at her.

"You've been through a lot in a very short amount of time, Olivia. I think you would really benefit from the time off. You need to heal from this before you start putting more pressure on yourself."

"But I'm an assistant manager. My boss needs me to work."

"Let's stop thinking about what other people need from you and start thinking about what you need. I would like you to have six weeks off."

"Six weeks?"

"Liv." My mum says from beside me. "This will be good for you."

"I'll also change your medication as well whilst you're here. The other one isn't working the way I would like it to, so I'm going to put you on something else."

"Ok," I look down at my hands.

"Olivia." Doctor Jones says to get my attention. "This is not your fault."

"I know," I offer her a small smile.

"No. I mean it. None of what happened to you is your fault. This type of behaviour is common in narcissistic relationships. None of his behaviour is your fault."

Everything I've managed to hold back today comes rushing out of me. "He wasn't always like this, you know?" My mum comes to hold me. "At the beginning, it was so good. I don't know where it all went wrong."

Doctor Jones hands me a box of tissues. "Olivia, I need you to hear me. His actions are his alone. You did nothing wrong. You're the victim here."

She continues talking to me about what she thinks is best for me, I don't try to argue with her anymore. She knows more about this kind of thing than I do. She doesn't understand that he only acted the way he did because I went against his wishes, though. By the time we leave the doctor's surgery, I have a prescription for a new medication, a referral for the mental health team and a sick note for six weeks off of work.

When we get home, I excuse myself to my bedroom. I need to call Cindy and let her know that I'll not be in for the next six weeks. She always gets frustrated when people have time off of work, hence why I never have a sick day, nor do I use all of my holiday days. It's not always because I'm worried about how she'll react, but because working keeps my head busy. When I have too much time to sit around and think about things, I end up spiralling.

Everything in my room reminds me of him, my bedding, my clothes, my old torn-up sofa. I perch myself on the arm of the chair he sat in so many times before and pull my phone out to call my boss. She answers on the second ring.

"Hello."

"Hi Cindy, it's Olivia."

"Olivia, is everything ok?" I can hear her type the code in for the staffroom door.

I rub my forehead with my spare hand. "Not really, no."

"Is there anything I can help with?"

"No. I had to go to the doctors today. They've signed me off for six weeks."

We spend the next fifteen minutes talking about what had happened and what the doctor would like me to do. She's very sympathetic and tells me to take all the time I need. I feel such relief that she hasn't got worked up about the length of time I need to have off. I tell her exactly the same things that I told the doctor, still leaving out the parts of the story that could land him in any danger. I may not want to be with him anymore, but I don't want him to suffer.

The rest of the day is spent with my mum. I don't leave her side once. We have lunch and dinner together. We watch TV, cuddled up on the sofa together. We don't really talk about anything that has happened. I'm grateful she doesn't bring it up.

When I'm alone in bed that night, I update the friends that I have left on what's happened today. Lily will be busy working, but Natalia has offered to be by my side whenever I need her there. I take her up on her offer, and tomorrow we'll be going for breakfast together.

That night, I dream of Jack. I dream of our first date when he took me for dinner. I dream about all the times we laughed together, all the times we talked about our future together, the children we would have, and the big house with a huge garden for them to play in. I dream about the first time he claimed me as his own, how gentle he was, how he was constantly asking me if things were ok. I dream about how perfect he was. He was such a gentleman.

Chapter 30

The following morning, I wake up early. I have a very long and super-hot shower and eat a small snack to line my stomach. I'm glad to have my appetite back, but my stomach is still very angry from all the violent throwing up sessions it has had to go through these last few days. I feel good today. Although we're only going for breakfast, I decide that I want to look good. Nat has seen me in so many states that she probably wouldn't bat an eyelid if I turned up in my PJs. Today is the first day of the rest of my life, though.

My hair has been curled. It's so long it still hangs below my breasts. I've pulled the top section back and have clipped it in place with a bow, the front pieces are loosely curled around my face. Makeup wise, I've applied a skin tint, enough coverage to even my skin tone, but it's light enough that you can still see my freckles through it. I've only applied mascara to my eyes.

When getting dressed, I must try on at least twenty different outfits. None made me feel good. In the end, I put on a pair of black tights and opt for my black skort. Tucked into it is a deep burgundy over-sized cable knit jumper. It's so big it hangs perfectly off of one shoulder. On my feet I have picked my knee-high black boots.

Everything about the way I look today is the opposite of how Jack liked me to look. He liked my eyeliner, he liked my hair up, he liked me covered head to toe. I'm still covered because of the wintry weather, but he would've had a heart attack if he saw me with my legs out. I snap a quick selfie in the mirror, upload it to my Instagram with the caption "Fresh start" and head out the door to meet Nat.

We each eat our breakfasts and decide to have a cocktail after for dessert. Ok, that's a lie. We have three each. It's turned into a boozy breakfast, something I'm starting to think we should make a tradition, because of the amount of fun we're having.

"Oi listen," Nat points her finger at me across the table, "that Lewis I work with has been messaging me basically daily asking me how you are. What am I meant to say to him?"

I give her my best-disgusted look. "Why does he care?"

She blows out of her lips, making the sound of a horse. "Fucked if I know."

"He could just ask me himself?" She winks at me from across the table. "Natalia. Absolutely not. Get that idea out of your head."

"Come on," she pouts at me, "you know the best way to get over someone is to get under someone else."

"It was definitely a man that made that saying up. No girl thinks that way."

"I think that way," her eyes bulge from her head, "I have an idea."

I overdramatically facepalm, "Fuck my life. Someone get this woman away from me."

"Lewis, hi." My head snaps up in her direction, she has her phone pinned against the side of her face.

I mouth no to her, but she waves me off with her hand.

"I was just having breakfast with Liv," she pauses, "how can you be this obsessed with her and not know her name?" She shakes her head at me like she can't believe that in the two times we've spoken, I haven't given him my name. "Anyway, they broke up," another pause, "well, you could add her on Facebook or follow her on Instagram and ask her yourself," she fist pumps. "Great idea, I'll arrange it. Bye."

"Arrange what?"

"Lewis is new to town, and he would like to go out."

"Natalia, I swear to god."

"Relax, Mum, it will be fun! Please," she bats her long black lashes at me.

"Do I have a choice?"

"Nope." She smiles as she chugs the rest of her cocktail.

We each drink another one when we then make the spontaneous decision to get a tattoo. Well Natalia makes the decision that I should get one. I already have a sternum tattoo, a half sleeve on my left arm, and a few other small ones dotted around various parts of my body. Does anyone remember when Selena Gomez got the semi-colon tattooed on her? Well, we decide that's what I'll get. It's symbolic to those who struggle mentally. It's for the people who thought their life would come to an end at some point, for people who have dealt with self-harm, depression, and other mental health issues. It symbolises that your story is not over. I think it's perfect. Once the tattoo is on my arm, then my new life can begin.

We contact the various tattoo artists in town until we find one who has space for right now before I back out. I'm the least spontaneous person I know. I believe everything is better when it has all been planned out.

The tattoo takes no longer than half an hour from start to finish. It's smaller than my others, but it has so much more meaning. My phone buzzes when we walk out of the tattoo studio.

Jade: Cindy told me why you are signed off. Hope you are ok.

WHAT.

"Oh my God." I stop in the middle of the street.

"What?" Nat grabs my phone from my hand. "She told her everything?"

Me: How much did she tell you?

Jade: She said you self-harmed because of everything that happened. She also said that she thinks it would be best for you to come back to work, to keep your mind off of it all.

My jaw is on the floor. *How could she do that to me?*

"You do know that she's not allowed to do that right?" Nat says to me.

"Why would she?"

"It doesn't matter why, Liv. She shouldn't have done it. You told her that in confidence."

She snatches my phone from my hand and starts typing a message.

Me: Harriet, it's Nat. Olivia's boss has told other members of staff all the things Liv told her in confidence. She can get done for that, right?

Mum: That bitch. Yes, she can.

"I can't go back there now. Like ever. They'll all look at me like I'm a victim, I don't want to be a victim anymore," I look to my friend.

"Then you quit."

"I worked so hard, though, Nat. I can't just throw all of that away."

"Yes, you can. I can speak to my boss and see if we have anything open at the moment. Just until you get back on your feet."

"I appreciate that, but I couldn't work there, Nat."

All of the confidence I felt this morning has now gone. I feel like a fragile shell of a human being. Who was I kidding, thinking I could just start over. I've lost my boyfriend, I've lost most of my friends, and I've now lost my job.

Nat continues to communicate with my mum, who is still off work, as she booked some extra holiday. They decide together that my mum will write a resignation letter and pack my uniform into a carrier bag, then Nat will meet her, and they will take it into the store together. I remove Cindy from all of my social media accounts, and I block her number. I've confided in this woman so many times, about so many personal things, and now I'm left wondering what else she has spread behind my back without my permission. She's a wolf in sheep's clothing.

Whilst the others are busy in the store, I look up the contact information for the head office and give them a call. I ask them to put me through to Debra, the regional manager of my store. I explain my situation to her.

"Olivia, I'm so sorry this has happened to you. We'll make sure Cindy is spoken to."

"Spoken to?" I practically spit down the phone.

"I understand you're frustrated, Olivia, but Cindy has been with us for many years, and we haven't had a complaint like this before." Her patronising voice sounds like nails down a chalkboard. "Please tell me if there is any way we can keep you with us?"

"The only way that I would stay with this company is if she's gone. I will not work with someone who believes it's acceptable to spread such personal news around."

"I'm really sorry, Olivia. But that's not something I can do. She is a very valued member of my team."

"And I'm not?"

"The truth is, it would be much easier for us to replace someone in your position than it would be to replace her."

"Easy to replace me!" I shout at her, "I run that store five, sometimes six days a week because she can't be bothered to drive over here. I do her job for her, and I'm not paid for that extra responsibility she puts on me."

"I hear what you're saying, but she is still the manager of multiple stores. She's been with us for twenty years now."

"So, you are telling me that you value her more than your other members of staff purely because she has been with the company longer? Not because of her work performance?"

"She would be too big a loss for us to."

I hang up. *Bitch.* The entire company is corrupt. My mum and Nat find me after they've dropped my uniform and resignation letter off. They said no one asked how I was. No one seemed bothered about me leaving. I tell them I've had no luck with the regional manager. My mum goes on to tell me I'm too good for them anyway. They don't deserve someone like me on their team. I'm pretty sure she has to say that though, isn't it what you do as a parent? She gives Nat a lift home and when I get home, I go straight upstairs to run a bath. The sharp objects have now returned to their original places, but I'm no longer tempted by them.

When I'm in the bath, I scroll through my social media, the photo I posted on Instagram got way more likes than I thought it would. That always happens, though, whenever you break up with someone and the desperate men find out, they're like vultures. As I click on the heart in the corner to clear the notifications, I notice I have a new follower. On closer inspection I realise it's Lewis.

A quick stalk through his social media tells me truly little about him. I know he's single, he has a four-year-old son, and he has a creepy obsession with his car. The shirtless pictures are certainly something to look at, though. I follow him back and lock my phone. I pick up the newest Meagan Brandy book and try to lose myself in it.

The first book of hers I read was Say You Swear, and it made me cry more than any book ever has. Her writing is so powerful. I love a book that makes you feel everything: happiness, sadness, butterflies.

I only manage the first two chapters when my phone buzzes from the floor beside the bath. I let out a grunt because I don't like being interrupted when I'm reading. When I pick it up it's a message from Lewis on Instagram. I get that giddy feeling in my stomach. Don't get me wrong, I'm not ready to open my heart up to another man yet, it's still too broken, but the attention is nice. Maybe Natalia was right.

Lewis: Hey, Nat told me you broke up with Jack. Are you ok?

Me: Not really, but time heals all wounds.

Lewis: It's ok to not be ok all the time you know.

Me: I seem to be not ok more than I am ok these days.

Lewis: Talk to me about it.

Me: About what?

Lewis: Everything that has happened. Tell me about it all.

I do. I'm not entirely sure why I do, but I do. I don't leave out a single detail. The way I have with the doctor and my mother, I tell him every single disgusting detail. Whilst I wait for his reply I get out of the now cold bath. I wrap the towel around myself and sit on the edge of the bath, biting the skin off my lip until it bleeds. It's a bad habit I can't seem to shake no matter how hard I try.

Lewis: I knew something wasn't right. When I saw him that first night, I didn't want to let you go home with him. If you had shown any sign of not wanting to go, I would have done anything to keep him away from you. You deserve someone who loves you for who you are, Olivia. Someone who thinks your worst flaws are things they cannot live without.

Me: It's funny you say that because I don't think I deserve anyone. If you tried to stop me going home with him that night everything would have been much worse.

Lewis: You're safe now, Olivia. No man will touch you or hurt you like that again.

We continue talking to each other late into the night. As nice as it is, there's still that voice in the back of my mind screaming at me to be careful. Things were like this with Jack in the beginning. He said all the right things and did all the right things. He lied about who he was until he knew I was trapped under his spell.

Chapter 31

After talking to Lewis for the last two weeks, I caved and let Natalia plan a night out. I'm feeling much better. I've had my first appointment with the mental health team, who have decided that they will offer me CBT starting in three weeks' time. It wasn't until I spoke to my uncle, who works for the NHS, that I realised how lucky I am to not have a long wait. Some people go months before they hear back from them. I can't think of anything worse. Imagine reaching out for help and then being made to wait. Having to struggle for months before someone has the time for you.

I've spent a lot of my time with my sister and my niece. I still have two weeks left of sick pay until my resignation letter runs out, and I have to look for a job. I am meant to be signed off for another two weeks after that, but honestly, I just want to get back to some kind of normality. I've tried my best not to waste the money I do have left, but whenever I see an adorable outfit, I can't help but buy it for Grace. Our very own little dolly.

Everyone has been amazing. My friends and family have come together and have been there to help me get through this rough patch. My mum still sleeps in my bed, on the nights I wake up screaming from a nightmare, and I still try to avoid going into town if I can help it. I will order everything I need online or ask someone else to pick stuff up for me. Tonight, will be the first time I've shown my face in public since that night Jack punched the wall, and my first time being in the club since I had that mental breakdown in front of everyone.

My hair is straight tonight, in a middle parting. I've tucked my face-framing pieces behind my ears. My hair is darker than it was all those months ago, the ginger hues are massively toned down, and it almost appears brown without the sun out to bleach it. I have done my makeup with a full coverage foundation, contoured to the max to show off my cheekbones. My sister is learning how to apply lash extensions, so I let her use me as a test run. For a first try, they look amazing. I still haven't used any eyeliner, only a small amount of brown shadow on my lids. The red lip is still there, though. I always feel like a red lip is such a power move.

Since the breakup, I've lost a lot of weight from the lack of eating and excessive throwing up, so I had to buy a new outfit last night. *Thank goodness for next-day delivery.* I got a black bodysuit. It's low cut with thin straps. It has a small lace trim around the incredibly low neckline, and in the detail of the lace are small, embroidered tulips. I have paired it with some black faux leather shorts. Although purple may be my favourite colour, most of my wardrobe is full of black and white clothing.

The girl in the mirror is someone I am starting to be proud of. She has been through a hell of a lot, and she's coming out the other side stronger than ever.

Nat, Lily, and I are meeting Lewis and his friends, George and Arthur at the pub. Lewis is definitely the best looking one out of his friendship group, although they all have blonde hair and blue eyes, like some kind of cult. We get there before them and grab a booth in the corner, we manage to have two drinks and a shot each before they arrive.

When Lewis locks eyes with me from across the room, I get butterflies in my stomach. He has been so kind and caring towards me since we started talking to each other. He knows I'm not ready for another relationship yet. I don't think I could commit to another person for a while, but he still checks in on me.

As he approaches the table, I wiggle out of the booth.

"Hey," I smile at him as he reaches out to wrap me up in his arms.

"You look beautiful," he whispers in my ear for only me to hear. "What are you all drinking then? I better get the first-round in."

"Are you not going to introduce us to your friends?" Nat raises her brow at him.

“Oh right, sorry.” He’s nervous. I can tell he is. “This is Arthur,” he points to the tallest member of his cult, “and this is George,” both offer us small nods before sitting beside Lily on one side of the booth.

“We will have a pitcher of sex on the beach for the three of us and a shot of Sourz each. Thanks.” Nat gives him a fake grin.

“Do you want me to come with you?” I ask him.

“No. You sit down. George can come with me,” he brushes his hand across my lower back.

When we have finished two more pitchers, we start to stumble towards the club. Lewis holds my elbow to get me to slow down and walk behind the rest of the group with him.

“How are you feeling?” Those blue eyes stare into mine. Lewis in uniform is yum, but Lewis in going-out attire is unbeatable. He is wearing a plain white T-shirt, which hugs his toned body in all the right places. He has paired it with a relaxed pair of light blue jeans. He has a chain around his neck and a large watch on one of his wrists.

“I’m ok.” *That’s a lie.*

“You don’t have to pretend with me, Olivia.” He nudges me with his shoulder.

“Ok. I’m terrified. Are you happy now?” I cock my head.

“No. Obviously not.”

I look up to the sky. “I just haven’t seen him since it all happened. I have no idea how he’s going to act if he sees me out. I blocked him on everything so he can’t contact me, and I’ve stayed hidden, so I don’t bump into him on my own.”

“You won't be on your own tonight. You have me.” He holds my hand in his. “None of us will let him hurt you.”

It doesn’t matter what anyone says to me in this moment. I am terrified.

The club is already packed by the time we get there, we spent longer than normal sitting in the pub talking to each other. Arthur was telling us all about his fiancé and daughter, George told us how he had his heart broken four years ago and has sworn off women ever since. Natalia drunkenly admitted to the table that she's not sure if she wants to be with her boyfriend anymore as he talks to her like crap. Lily was the quietest, but she still opened up about how she had just not found the right person for her yet. Lewis told us about his ex-girlfriend and how well they get along whilst co-parenting their son. They had been in a relationship since school, and one day, they just realised they didn't love each other anymore. I kept my speech short and sweet. Four of us around the table already knew everything that happened, but it's much harder to talk about in person.

It's not long until I notice Lewis go stiff beside me on the dance floor. When I turn to look at him, I know he's here. Nat turns to look behind her where Lewis is staring, and her shoulders rise. "Let's go outside," I shout above the music.

I have to practically drag Lewis from the dance floor. When we are outside, I go to head to the table in the corner but freeze. *The same table I met him at.*

"There's one over here," Nat pulls my arm, reading my mind, "I can't believe he is actually here."

"Why wouldn't he be?" They can't really be that shocked that he's here.

"He has some nerve," Lily says under her breath.

"Does he, though?" I put my elbows on the table and rest my chin in my hands. "We all knew it was likely that he would be here tonight. The man lives here."

"Boy," Lewis corrects me. "He is not a man."

"Why are you defending him, Liv?" Nat says from across the table.

"What? I'm not."

"Yes, you kind of are. He should be locked up, and the key should be thrown away. He did awful things to you, and you still think it's ok that he is out here in the real world living his life."

"I never said that, did I. I just knew he would be here."

"Olivia. Wake up, for God sake."

"I don't need to hear this right now," I snatch my bag and drink from the table and head inside on my own.

I don't get far before Jack finds me. He corners me at the bottom of the stairs. He looks tired. Those deep brown eyes are filled with sadness. Sadness because I left him. I broke his heart.

"Can we talk?" He tucks my hair behind my ear. The small touch sends a shock through my entire body.

"Jack," I look up at him through my lashes, "there really is nothing else to say."

"Come on, Liv." He traces my bottom lip with his thumb. "It doesn't have to end like this. Just hear me out."

"It does. We can't be what we used to be. Too much has happened."

"We don't have to be what we used to be, we can be better."

"Jack…"

"You broke my heart," he looks into my eyes, "I don't know who I am without you."

"Then use this time to find out. I'm so sorry, Jack, but I can't go back to that. This is what's best for both of us. Time apart to focus on ourselves."

"It's because of him, isn't it?" He frowns at me. "You don't love me anymore because you've already moved on."

"What are you on about?" I pull his hand from my face and hold it. "I never fell out of love with you. I promised I would love you forever, and I meant it. But I have to love you from a distance. You have to let me go."

Lewis clears his throat from beside us, and Jack tenses up. His head turns at an alarmingly slow pace until he is facing him.

"You. You got in her head. You poisoned her against me."

"I did nothing, Jack. She made the choice by herself."

He looks back at me and snatches his hand from mine. "You fucking whore. You just couldn't wait, could you? You're already fucking someone else. He'll soon get bored of your mind games. You are nothing, Olivia, nothing without me."

I say nothing. Any sadness I found in his eyes five minutes ago has been replaced by anger. He has used me as his verbal punching bag for so long that I don't have the energy to fight back anymore. I shake my head at him and try to push past him, but he grabs my arm.

"Let me go, Jack."

"You are so fucking desperate. You'll pay for what you've done to me."

"Let. Me. Go."

Everything that happens next seems to happen in slow motion. I can see him pull his arm back, his hand turn into a fist. Lewis is stood behind me, so he can't stop what is about to happen, he promised he wouldn't be able to hurt me anymore, but how can he save me if he can't see what's about to happen. My eyes are fixed on Jack's as his fist collides with my face. He sends me flying into the staircase, where I hit my head on the step. Then everything goes black.

Chapter 32

Before...

They're fighting again.

Rose and I tried to run upstairs, but he dragged us back down. We're cuddled into each other on the old sofa now. It's nearly Christmas, everyone should be happy, but I have learnt already that this man never is.

Our living room has been decorated with ceiling decorations, all red and gold. Our Christmas tree looks beautiful. All of the lights twinkle like hundreds of tiny stars. We helped decorate the tree this year. My mum told me that I am old enough to help with the decorations. It was the best day ever. Me and Rose helped her with everything.

He's shouting at her in the kitchen. I don't understand why we aren't allowed to go upstairs. He threw us both on the sofa before he went back into the kitchen to continue shouting. Our sofa is green with flowers dotted all over it. I'm unsure how long we have had it for, but I hope we get to keep it forever. I love flowers.

With a loud slam of the door, our mum comes back into the living room. Her hair is all messed up, and she is crying. She is so sad. He makes her so sad. I wish we could run away. She is saying something to us, but I can't hear her over the ringing in my ears.

He's in the front room now, pointing and shouting in her face. I want to tell him to stop. I want to help her, but I can't move. She is trying to push him away from her, but he has gripped hold of her shoulders so tightly she can't get away.

He starts shaking her violently. Rose is screaming. I can tell because her mouth is wide open, and her eyes are full of tears. She needs to be quiet. She has to stop screaming. She is only going to make it worse.

It all happens so fast.

He pushes her so hard she falls into our Christmas tree. We all worked so hard on making it perfect. It goes down with her.

The worst part is that I know this is only the beginning.

Chapter 33

One month later...

I have finally secured another job. The local clothing store was looking for a key holder. It's a step down from what I was doing previously, but the pay is so much better. Plus, working with clothes every day is my idea of heaven. After a week of working there, I have abused my staff discount after every single shift. My wardrobe has never looked so good. It will certainly do for now whilst I figure out what it is I would like to do long term.

It's been a month since the last time I went out. I've told my friends that I won't be going out for a while. I woke up in hospital alone. They called my mum, but it took her a while to get up to me. I had a nice black eye and concussion, but other than that, I was ok. Jack has been banned from the club, and the police told me I could press charges. I honestly just wanted it all over with, so I told them I didn't want to. When I was laid in that hospital bed, I made the decision that I never wanted to see him or speak to him ever again. Having to talk to the police about it all would be going against what I wanted. I don't want to relive it all.

I have apologised to my mum a million times. I feel like I let her down by getting involved with someone who was exactly the same as my birth dad. Every time, she tells me that it wasn't my fault, that people like him are professionals at what they do. I still hope that one day, he does meet a girl, they settle down, and they have a family together. I refuse to believe that he's all bad. There has to be some good in everyone.

When I raised my concerns with my old manager to the people at the very top of the food chain, they gave me a nice compensation package. Apparently, threatening to take them to court was enough for them to shit themselves. I decided that was enough for me. It was another thing I just wanted to move on from and forget about. I haven't spoken to Jade since that day, mainly because I don't want her going back to Cindy and updating her on my life, but also because she hangs around with Dylan a lot.

After that night, Nat did go down to her boyfriend's and broke up with him. She found proof he was, in fact, having an affair again. She said that I inspired her, and she feels like she can start over now.

As I finish locking up the shop, I turn to find Lewis leaning against a lamppost.

"What are you doing here?" I ask him.

He texted me the day after, apologising because he couldn't stop what happened. He tried to come to the hospital with me, but they wouldn't let him. We have spent some time together. I refuse to call them dates because I still don't think that I'm ready for that. But when two people spend time together at a restaurant, it is usually a date.

"I got you something."

"You did?" I frown at him.

"Yup." He makes a point of overdoing it on the p. "They're in my car."

"And where would your car be?"

"Follow me." He reaches his hand out, and I link mine to his.

"You really drove all the way here to give me something?"

"It's only a twenty-minute drive, Olive. Calm down." Olive happens to be the nickname he chose for me. I asked everyone to stop calling me Liv. I've spent the last month doing everything in my power to remove every trace of Jack from my life.

We walk hand in hand to his car, he opens the boot, and I gasp. "How did you know?"

"The top you wore out that night."

Tears fill my eyes as I throw my arms around his neck. "Thank you."

When I pull myself together, I release my hold on his neck and run my hands over the twenty-three bunches of tulips in his boot. One bunch for every year I've been alive.

"I'll wait for you. I don't care how long it takes. I'll wait for you, Olivia." He tucks my hair behind my ear.

"I'm so sorry."

"Why are you sorry?" He frowns

"You shouldn't have to wait for me."

"You never have to apologise to me." He kisses my forehead. "It's my choice to wait."

When Lewis drove me home, he had to help me carry all the flowers into my house. My mum got home soon after, and I saw the panic in her eyes. I reassured her that I wasn't rushing into anything. I'm enjoying this time to get to know myself again. There is nothing more powerful than a woman that loves herself.

I don't recognise the girl I was a year ago. So much has changed in such a short amount of time. But I am happy.

Lily: He got you all of them?

Me: Yep.

Nat: You better not get a boyfriend. I was just starting to like our band of strong, independent women.

Me: You're so dramatic. He knows I'm not ready for that yet. I'm all yours, I promise.

Nat: FYI, Lil, I'm not sharing.

Lily: Ew.

When I'm ready for bed that night, I take a second to look around my new room. My mum and dad decided we should swap rooms shortly after what happened. A fresh start in life means a new room as well, according to them. I've not long finished decorating it. I have a new bed, wardrobe, and set of drawers, all of them are white. The opposite of what I had before. The bedding on my bed at the moment is covered with pink and white flowers. The pink is so bright it almost burns my eyes to look at it. The sofa is long gone, it was the first thing we got rid of when we were moving my stuff down the hall. Instead, I now have a small desk, which has been turned into a makeup station. The drawers are full of makeup, skincare, and various hair products. You name it, and I have it.

There's a canvas hanging above my bed. My sister gifted it to me a few days ago. It's a photo of me and Grace, the day she was born. She told me that if I'm ever having a bad day, I just need to look at it and remember who I'm fighting my demons for. There isn't anything I wouldn't do for that little girl.

Me: I had to use pint glasses in the end.

Lewis: I meant what I said, Olive. I will wait an eternity if it means I get to end up with you.

Me: How very dramatic.

Lewis: You love it.

I lay in bed and look around at all of the vases and glasses dotted around my room, full of purple tulips. I think back to the time Jack asked me what my favourite flower was and how he acted when I told him. Lewis never even asked me. He just knows me.

Tomorrow is my second therapy session. I've come so far already. They're so impressed with my progress. I finally feel like I'm able to think clearly again. My mind is no longer crowded. I understand now that everything that happened to me was not my fault. As well as I have done in therapy, it hasn't been easy. The first session ended with me in tears. The actual therapy is so mentally exhausting, but I know the long-term effects will be worth it, as long as I keep putting in the work.

This last year of my life has been crazy. I'm so grateful for the people that have stuck by me through it all.

I fall asleep with them in mind.

Loves Dark Facade Playlist -

Narcissist – Lauren Spencer Smith

The Smallest Man Who Ever Lived – Taylor Swift

THE GREATEST – Billlie Eilish

traitor – Olivia Rodrigo

Be Alright – Dean Lewis

Chloe or Sam or Sophia or Marcus – Taylor Swift

So Long, London – Taylor Swift

You're Losing Me – Taylor Swift

Therapy – All Time Low

Goodbye – Avril Lavigne

TV – Billie Eilish

Happier Than Ever – Billie Eilish

Lose You To Love Me – Selena Gomez

my tears ricochet – Taylor Swift

Bad Life – Sigrid & Bring Me The Horizon

Would've, Could've, Should've - Taylor Swift

Should've Said No – Taylor Swift

Fireworks – You Me At Six

Island of the Misfit Boy – Front Porch Step

Acknowledgements

A massive thank you to my partner in crime, Carl, for being the most supportive partner a woman could ask for. Thank you for being my biggest cheerleader and encouraging me to be the best version of myself. Without you I don't think I would have ever had the courage to write this book. You are the most amazing boyfriend and dad, and we are so lucky to have you in our lives. Thank you for holding my hand through everything.

To Mum and Dad, thank you for raising me to be this very strong, stubborn, and determined woman. Mum, if we had never had the conversation where we were joking about turning my life experiences into novels, Olivia would have never existed. You have both supported me through so much in my life and I am forever in your debt.

To the woman who this book has been dedicated to, my Nan. You taught me to chase my dreams and never give up on life, even when things get tough. I know you would be so proud of me if you could be here with us, my book would be at the top of your bookshelf alongside all of your Danielle Steel ones.

My incredible friends Tamsin, Claire, and Emma. Thank you for proofreading chapters, editing, helping pick the title, book cover and cheering me on every step of the way. Thank you for also being there for me over the years and helping me through some of the toughest moments of my life. You are the type of friends every girl wishes for, and I wouldn't be where I am today without you.

To Helen Jackson, you will not expect to see your name in here, but it's only right you are included. Thank you for believing in me even when I couldn't believe in myself. You have supported me through several dark battles with my mental health and have always helped me come out the other side stronger. Thanks to you I was able to finish writing this novel and will be able to write many more in the future.

Thank you to anybody who picks up this book and follows Olivia's journey. My hope with this book was to highlight narcissistic behaviours and relationships, and to hopefully help someone in the same position as Olivia realise that there is a better life out there. You can always reach out to someone and get the help you need. You are not alone.

A final thank you to mine and my friend's ex-boyfriends, without you we wouldn't have these amazing stories about self-discovery, independence, and friendship to tell.

Printed in Dunstable, United Kingdom

65888530R00129